IN JACOB'S ARMS

ALICIA RADES

To Rheanna, who has always supported my writing.

CHAPTER ONE

WHEN I WAS A KID, I fell in love with film, but art is the only thing I've ever fallen for. I've never believed I could fall for a man. I've watched women on the screen fall head over heels for men so many times, but I've never envisioned that for myself. Every guy I meet thinks he knows me because he recognizes my face. But I'm not the character I played in movies.

Even if I was, I've never played the love interest—and I'm certain I never will.

Men love the *idea* of me, yet they never take the time to get to know who I really am. So how can they really love me?

I've long since accepted the idea that my life isn't a romantic comedy. I haven't thought about dating in ages. Which is why I'm reluctant when my roommate wants to set me up.

Juliet stumbles out of her bedroom, hair a mess and

makeup smudged across her face. I move around the kitchen after pouring myself a cup of coffee, lounging in my usually Saturday morning attire. My baggy sweats and oversized t-shirt cover my small frame.

Despite her tired appearance, Juliet is still stunning. She actually has hips and boobs, and she's about five inches taller than me with long, slender model legs. Her lengthy blonde hair cascades down her back to make her even more gorgeous. She's the kind of woman who turns heads and makes every guy want her and every girl jealous. She could easily be a model, although she never pursued the career.

"Long night?" I ask.

She looks at me, rubs her eyes, and says in a tired tone, "Opening nights for exhibits always go late, and it's even worse when I'm in charge of them."

It's not that the reception itself goes late, but Juliet always stays later, admiring the artwork and celebrating with her coworkers. This only happens when she doesn't end up going home with a guy, though judging by her appearance, she slept alone last night.

Juliet's an art geek and has art easels and beautiful paintings strewn across the apartment. While she doesn't display her work often, she loves art and works as an assistant curator at a small gallery just a few blocks from our apartment. The way she's working her way up in her career astounds me, and she's even managed to get one of her paintings accepted in an upcoming show at a different local gallery.

Juliet takes a deep, refreshing yawn, extending her

arms above her head and stretching to her tip toes. She comes down from her stretch, and her face lights up. A big, god-awful smile forms across it. She leans her elbows on the breakfast bar and swings her hips from side to side, pivoting on one foot. She stares at me with that dreadful smile, and I know she's just waiting for me to ask what's up so that she can reveal her dirty little secret.

My eyebrows come together. *Does* she have someone in her bedroom?

"What?" I ask. "Did you get laid or something?"

I lean against the counter and take a sip of my coffee. It wouldn't surprise me, and it wouldn't be anything new. She's currently in between men, so I suppose she's in need of some.

Pot, meet kettle.

"No!" she squeaks. "Why would you say that?"

"Your smile is kind of scaring me." *And it is so like you,* I think, although I don't say it out loud.

She giggles. "I didn't get laid, but I *do* have news for you. Rather, an offer."

I stick out my right hip and place my hand upon it. My face transforms into a glare that clearly says, *Oh, no. What do you want me to do this time?*

"No, no," she insists as she straightens up, her hands outstretched in a way that implies I should calm down. "Just hear me out."

"All right..." I turn away from her and begin preparing myself toast.

"There's this guy I work with," Juliet begins. "He just

started working at the gallery helping with the exhibits and stuff, and I've gotten to know him pretty well. We got to chatting a bit more last night at the reception. He's, like, totally not my type, though. Somehow, we ended up on the subject of you—"

I spin around and stop her. Stunned, I stare up at her past the frames of my glasses. "Me? What were you talking about me for?"

"I was telling him about my paintings in the apartment, and I mentioned I had a roommate." She waves her hand like it's nothing. "Anyway, when I mentioned your name, he had no idea who you were—no indication of familiarity whatsoever—so I thought this would be a great opportunity for you to meet someone who doesn't have any preconceived notions of who you are. If you'll accept, I can set you two up on a blind date!"

I raise my brows at her as if she's mad. "Juliet, I thought we agreed that you wouldn't set me up on any more blind dates."

She's done this before, and each date has turned into a disaster.

The longest record I have before my blind date says, *Hey, I know you*, is eight minutes and thirty-two seconds. After college, Juliet was constantly trying to set me up on blind dates, but the guys always seemed to know who I was, which in turn caused them to act weird around me. It became difficult to enjoy dating at all, which is why I stopped accepting her invitations.

Dating has never been my strong suit. There's nothing

extraordinary about me, but everyone seems to think I'm some superior being. I started acting when I was four. By the time I was seven, I landed myself three major roles in hit films. Although I stopped acting after filming the third movie, people still know who I am.

I sometimes want to just scream, "It was 20 years ago. Get over it!"

Honestly, my acting career feels like a whole different lifetime. That's not who I am anymore, yet people still use it against me as if it defines me.

Perhaps people still recognize me because I never seemed to grow out of my childish appearance. I never grew hips, and I barely have boobs. Hell, I look more like a twelve-year-old than a twenty-six-year-old. Plus, my signature pouty bottom lip that made me so cute in my days of acting never seemed to recess to normal. I still style my hair with straight-across bangs because frankly, it's the only way to hide my giant forehead. The only thing that has changed about me is my height and the gradual darkening of my auburn hair.

It's because of my past and the fact that so many people recognize me that I have a difficult time accepting Juliet's latest offer. I just don't want to go through that experience again.

She comes around the counter. "Come on, Siobhan," she begs, bending her knees and giving a bit of a hop. "When was the last time you went out on a date?"

"I don't know," I lie. The truth is, I haven't been on a date in over two years, and I'm in desperate need of some intimate contact—and the vibrator that lives in my night-stand doesn't count.

"You're always complaining about how there aren't any good guys out there because they look at you like you're still a child," she argues. "This guy is so great for you, and he doesn't have any biased ideas about who you are. I want to see you with someone for once, Siobhan. I want you to be happy. He's a great guy."

She has a point, but I'm not keen on the idea. "He probably just doesn't recognize how to pronounce my name. If you don't spell it out for him, he won't get the connection."

It's true. No one knows how to say my name. It should be spelled S-h-i-v-a-h-n or something, but that's what Irish names will get you. "He'd probably recognize me once he saw me. I *do* still look like I did when I was five."

"No, he won't," she promises. "I *casually* mentioned your movies, and he's never seen any of them. He doesn't know you."

I throw my hand up. "Now he does because you told him."

"No," she insists. "I casually mentioned it. I didn't say that you were in them!"

I stand in silence for a moment, almost considering the idea. If there is a guy out there, one who Juliet thinks is good for me and who doesn't think of me as the same little girl I once was, perhaps there's a chance with him.

I quickly shake off the notion. Juliet isn't that great at detecting the perfect couple. Hell, she can't even land *herself* the perfect guy. How is she supposed to find the perfect one for me?

As I contemplate this idea further, my toast pops, scaring me. I jump, and my coffee sprays out of its mug and onto my t-shirt. I slam my cup on the counter a bit harder than I should have and turn to grab the towel that hangs off the handle on the stove.

"Pleeeease," Juliet begs again, elongating the vowels.

I tilt my head and glare at her over my shoulder. She's leaning against the counter again, biting her lip impatiently.

"I'd really rather not," I tell her. Still, a thought in the back of my mind surfaces. What if this is my chance to meet a decent guy who won't judge me for my past?

I let the thought fall almost instantly. No. It hasn't happened before. What would make now any different, especially with Juliet's judge of character?

"Come on," Juliet says. "You can't stay single forever."

My heart gives a painful jolt at her words, but I don't let it show. I frown at her. "Maybe I want to be single."

Ha! If only that were the truth.

"It couldn't hurt," she presses.

I glower a moment longer before turning my head away from her and throwing down the towel. I don't want to have to deal with her ridiculous smile and constant pleading, and I know she won't stop until I agree.

"Fine," I relent, but I don't look at her.

She and I both know that I'm much overdue for a date.

My heart begins to race the moment I answer, but I'm not entirely sure why. I can't be *excited*.

I begin buttering my toast, my back still to her. "Tell me when and where, and I'll be there."

I spin around as I take an angry bite from my toast, except I rip off more than I intend, and I struggle to get the rest of the bite in my mouth. Juliet giggles at me, and I laugh along.

"I have to go change," I chuckle, gesturing to the fresh coffee stain on my shirt.

Juliet embraces me, though she's careful to avoid the coffee stain. "I'm so happy for you, Siobhan. Maybe for once you'll be in a real relationship."

Gee, thanks for the kind words, Juliet.

I free myself from her grasp and head to my room to get ready for the day.

I really hope this date doesn't end in disaster.

CHAPTER TWO

MY ROOM IS SMALL, just big enough for a double bed, nightstand, dresser, and a computer desk. My walls are bare compared to the rest of the apartment, which Juliet has practically turned into her own art gallery with her favorite paintings and photographs, both of her own work and of other artists. Most of the photos in my room are of me standing next to someone else—my mom, my sister, and Juliet.

I slip out of my pajamas and pull a tank top and shorts out of my drawer and put them on. At my dresser, I take my glasses off and place my contacts in my eyes. I pause briefly, staring back at myself in the mirror. I take a moment to study my high cheek bones, bright eyes, and soft skin, yet I find myself cursing my pale complexion and flat chest.

I tear my gaze from the mirror and toss my hair up in a high ponytail. I don't bother with my makeup because I'm not going anywhere. It's the weekend, but even so, I don't usually leave the apartment during the day. I typically sit on my computer working with clients on web design. Yep, that's what I'm using my graphic design degree for, and no matter what anyone tells you about web designers, I love my job. I'm my own boss and don't have to take shit from anyone.

Well, that's not true. Clients give me shit sometimes, but most of the time they're easy to work with.

I exit my bedroom and return to Juliet. She has her cell phone pressed to her ear, but I'm not entirely sure who she's speaking with.

"Awesome. Okay. She'll be there," she says, then hangs up. "You're set for Wednesday night at Michelle's at seven o'clock."

Michelle's is a restaurant not far from here, but I'm surprised. It always seems so fancy and expensive when I walk by, although I've never been inside.

"How do you know I'm not busy?" I tease.

"Oh, sorry," she apologizes with a smile. "Are you doing anything Wednesday night?"

Juliet knows that I never go out without her, so if she's not doing anything Wednesday night, she already knows that I'm not.

"No," I admit.

"Well, you are now. I've ordered you one romantic night with the beautiful Jacob Bishop."

God, I only hope he's beautiful.

Juliet turns and heads toward her bedroom.

I stop her. "Juliet?"

She pivots to look at me, but I can't read her expression.

"How will I know it's him? If what you say is true and he really doesn't recognize me, he won't know who I am, either."

"Oh," she says, like she already knows the answer but just forgot to tell me. "He'll be wearing a black cashmere sweater over a lavender collared shirt, and you'll be wearing that black single-strapped dress you wore the last time we went dancing."

That thing! But that's my sexy look-at-me dress. I don't want to look that desperate on the first date.

"Juliet," I begin to protest, but she interrupts me.

"Siobhan, I told him that's what you'll be wearing. You look hot in it; it'll be fine."

"Fine," I agree. I say I don't take shit from anyone, but I have a hard time disagreeing with Juliet. She's been my best friend since college, and we're practically sisters. I look up to her, and I can't ever seem to win an argument with her.

I remember meeting her for the first time. I had just moved to New York City, ready to start working on my degree. I was seated at my desk early for my first day of freshman English, determined to do my best that semester. She sauntered into the room and plopped down in the seat next to me, her hair swaying and looking as gorgeous as ever. I was intimidated at first by the way she carried herself and by her beauty.

"I will *not* put up with this shit," she said under her breath.

I couldn't help but stare at her, amazed by this woman who seemed so beautiful and strong.

"Are you okay?" I asked.

Her eyebrows knitted together in tension. "No, I am not okay. My roommate is a bitch."

Immediately, we had something in common. I wasn't too thrilled about my roommate either, who already had two different guys stay in our dorm room over the weekend. When she thought I was asleep, they'd make out on the loft next to mine. At least, I told myself they were *just* making out. I was not prepared for this.

"I'm not happy with mine, either," I told her.

"Maybe *we* should room together," she said with an edge of sarcasm before bending to her backpack to retrieve her book.

I sat there for a moment pondering the idea. This girl seemed a much better choice for me.

"I'm sure you'd be easier to get along with," I said in a light-hearted tone.

Her head popped back up from below the desk, and she stared into the distance as if she had a wonderful idea, but she quickly regained herself.

"Are you busy after this class? Maybe we could grab a bite to eat," she offered, and my stomach growled at the thought, reminding me that I hadn't eaten all day.

"Sounds great," I agreed.

Once Juliet got to know me a bit better, she invited me to switch rooms, and we'd been roommates ever since.

"Speaking of my dancing dress..." I say, pulling myself from my memory. "We really need another night out."

"Of course," she agrees. "You're still coming to the art show in two weeks when they display my painting, aren't you?"

"I wouldn't miss it for the world," I promise. "Maybe we can go out dancing that night to celebrate."

"Sure," she agrees. "I'll be really busy the next few weeks, so we probably won't have time together until then."

I'm relieved that we're finished talking about the blind date, and I begin cleaning our apartment to distract myself. Luckily Juliet stops harping on me, and the subject doesn't come up again for the rest of the day.

God, I'm nervous about dating again.

———

Wednesday approaches with unease. I continuously find my mind wandering off from my task, daydreaming about what this guy is like. While eating breakfast on Sunday, I catch myself staring off into the distance for so long that my entire bowl of cereal becomes far too soggy to eat. When I'm at my computer later, I accidentally create a six-page document because my elbow is rested on the space bar, my chin in my hand.

Sometimes I think he won't be any different from the

other guys I've dated— awkward, uninterested in who I really am, asks too many questions about my childhood. Other times, I fantasize about walking into Michelle's and falling upon the perfect guy. Problem is, I don't want to get my hopes up just to have them crushed.

I settle on the idea that he's probably pretty average. Perhaps if I believe this until Wednesday, my daydreams will set me up for the most likely scenario.

Except... what exactly did Juliet mean when she said that he's perfect for me, and why *hasn't* he seen any of my movies? Did he grow up without a TV? Maybe he's from another country. England, I hope, because those men have damn-fine accents.

There I go again, glamorizing this guy I've never met.

Perhaps I'm just too central to my past that I can't see reality. Maybe there are just people in the world who never cared to watch a movie I was in. It seems like everyone has seen at least one of them. I mean, people refer to *Celina the Detective* and *Taking Reservations* as classics.

The first movie I was in is about a little girl named Celina who gets bored and starts investigating the neighborhood. She's one of those kids who thinks she has the high-tech gadgets and starts dressing like Sherlock Holmes. In the end, she saves her elderly neighbor after a heart attack since she's always in everyone's business. People still call me Celina to this day.

As for the second film, I played the role of Suzan, the daughter of Amanda, played by the stunning and still popular Elizabeth River. In the movie, Amanda and her daughter move to New York City from a rural area. Struggling to get by, Amanda opens a restaurant, and the movie follows them along their journey.

These two films were big hits, but the third wasn't so much. *Beyond the Meadow* is about Sarah, who has nothing to do on summer vacation. For something to interest her, she begins exploring the family estate and heads beyond the meadow. There, she finds the land of the faeries, and they crown her queen. Homesick, she returns to her parents, but since she believes it was a dream, she never goes back until she's older and visits the estate again. In the end, the faeries cheer for their returned queen.

I stopped acting after the third film because the industry had become overwhelming. I hadn't worked with anyone my age, and all I wanted was to be a kid. I became exhausted by the attention and limelight, and I'm glad I got out when I did.

People like to glamourize my childhood, but it wasn't all perfect. I mean, I didn't just get things handed to me. I started out acting in commercials just like everyone else. My first gig was a cereal commercial, but the roles didn't just start coming as some people might believe. I worked my ass off in acting class to get all the techniques perfect, and I spent most of my free time studying scripts and attending auditions.

My parents didn't spoil me, either. If I wanted to act, they were going to make me put in all the effort on my own to do it—with the exception of transportation. And I did.

They took me to countless auditions before landing my first role, and I had several rejections in between each movie.

When filming for *Beyond the Meadow* ended, I knew I was done acting. It wasn't my thing anymore. Web designing is my passion, and I'd much rather create beautiful web pages than stand in front of the camera performing the same scene over and over again all day.

But damn it, why hasn't this guy heard of any of my movies? The more I think about it, the more of a mystery he is to me, and it fascinates me.

Isn't this what I want, a man who doesn't judge me for my past? I can't seem to set my mind straight to decide on an answer. The mystery annoys the hell out of me.

In anticipation of the date, I try to get more out of Juliet on Tuesday night.

"What's he like?" I ask.

She smiles, looking up from her canvas that she's working on. "I can't tell you, Siobhan. You'll have to figure that out yourself. I already divulged his name. I'm not telling you any more about him. That's the point of a blind date."

"Just tell me how hot he is," I beg.

"Come on, Siobhan. He doesn't know anything about you. It's only fair that you go in not knowing anything about him."

"What color are his eyes?"

"Siobhan Spencer," she teases, "are you actually getting excited for a date?"

That statement alone stops my inquiries. I don't want to give this one to Juliet by admitting that I'm a bit excited. Hell, I don't even want to admit it to myself.

I go to bed dreaming about the next day, my nerves shaking throughout my body while my excitement grows. Am I actually looking forward to this? Is Siobhan Spencer enthusiastic about her blind date?

If I'm speaking honestly, yes. Yes, I'm excited to finally have a date again after not being involved with anyone for two years. I want to talk to someone new, and not just a girl from my yoga class or a bartender at a club. I want to have a real conversation with a real man.

Of course, I can't admit this to Juliet. In truth, I'm somewhat glad that she found someone for me.

I'm just hoping beyond hope that I won't be disappointed.

CHAPTER THREE

I WAKE EARLY on Wednesday morning to prepare for my yoga class, which I take every Monday, Wednesday, and Friday to help relieve stress and maintain my flexibility.

I dress in my yoga pants and tank top, and I avoid the mirror as I prepare for the day. I grab my yoga mat, then head out the door, locking it behind me. I'm not in a hurry, and I'm a bit early, so I stop at the coffee shop along the way and grab myself a small cappuccino. I need it if I'm going to get anywhere today.

I enter the studio and quietly join my classmates, spreading my yoga mat near the center of the room. I sit upon it cross-legged and close my eyes, focusing my attention on the sounds in the room as more people shuffle into the yoga studio.

Normally I would talk to my friends Jasmine or Abby, but today I block everyone out.

I breathe in. I breathe out. I focus on my body and prepare myself for the session, but I find my mind wandering more than usual. Mostly, I can't get this mysterious man out of my head.

Once everyone is settled in and the clock hits six-thirty, our instructor Leanna enters the room. Her bare feet are quiet on the hardwood floor, and she floats with grace to the front center of the studio. Leanna carefully positions her yoga mat on the floor and sits on it. For a few moments, she's silent, taking in deep breaths and releasing them so that we can all hear.

"Good morning," she greets in a quiet, peaceful manner. "Today, we're going to focus on our breathing and really getting in tune with our bodies. Let's start out with some breathing exercises." Leanna presses a button on her speakers, initiating the calm, soothing music that fills the room for the rest of the session.

As she guides us through the breathing techniques, I once again find my mind wandering. Should I really wear that black dress tonight? And what should I do with my hair? Should I go with the red lipstick or not?

Leanna takes us further into our yoga poses, guiding us to downward-facing dog, through Chaturanga, and to some more advanced poses. When she advises us to take a rest in child's pose, I find myself stuck there. My body refuses to move, and I rest my forehead on the mat. As I try focusing on my breathing and my body as she directs, I discover that the task is quite difficult, and my muscles forget how to relax. I'm grateful when we finish in corpse pose. I quickly leave the room, my anxiety worse than when I walked in.

If anything, I get even more edgy over the next twelve hours as seven o'clock approaches.

I spend my day working on web development for clients, and I take breaks to update my blog and post a few messages to my followers, but I'm again trapped in low-productivity mode. God, I don't even know this guy and he's already affecting my performance.

When five o'clock rolls around, my stomach begins to flutter, and I attempt to fight it, not willing to admit that I'm actually looking forward to this. Damn Juliet Lane for making me feel this way. It's not her responsibility.

God, why am I even going on this date? I should go meet guys on my own, not rely on Juliet to find someone for me.

I start getting ready for my date early. I experiment with my hair a few different ways, but in the end, I decide to curl my hair and leave it down. I gaze at my reflection in approval, but for a final touch, I style my bangs to the right side and coat them in a mist of hairspray to make them stay. There. That makes me look a bit more mature.

I give myself dark brown eye shadow, rosy red cheeks, and bright red lipstick. I check the mirror for one last glance at my date look. Damn, I look really hot when I try. I know this is true, but I'm still trying to figure out a way to push in my sharp chin and pouty bottom lip.

I dress in my sleek single-shoulder black dress and slip

on a pair of high heels. When I return to the living room where Juliet is sitting with her laptop, she gapes at me.

"Ho-ly crap," she says slowly.

"What?" I ask, running my fingers through the ends of my hair. "Did I do something wrong?"

"No. Siobhan Spencer, you did *everything* right." She rises from the couch and circles around me, trying to get a good look from every angle. "Girl, you are hot!"

"That's kind of what I was going for," I say, and she nods in approval. "Well, I guess I'm off, then."

She gives me that cheesy grin again and bends down to embrace me. "Have a great time, Siobhan. I know you'll like him."

I grab my purse and exit the apartment, walking slowly to the restaurant. When I enter Michelle's, I'm grateful that the restaurant is small, although the enormous mirror that spans the wall to my left makes the room seem larger than it really is. The restaurant is filled with earthy tones and has a happy ambiance that hits me when I walk through the door. The delicious scent of pasta sauce touches my nose, and I realize that I haven't eaten all day. My stomach growls.

I check my phone. It's seven-oh-seven. I note the exact time and then slip my cell phone back into my purse.

I scan the tables. My gaze falls upon a lone man wearing a cashmere sweater over a lavender collared shirt. I was skeptical about how the outfit would look when Juliet told me about it, but this guy really pulls it off.

He sees me, and our eyes meet. With a wave of his hand, he gestures to me.

The way he gazes at me is odd. It really is like he's seeing me for the first time, and there's no look of shock in his eyes as if he recognizes me. I'm not used to it. This small detail alone intensifies my intrigue. Juliet was right. This guy doesn't know anything about me, and it makes me want to get to know him even more.

"Just one?" the host asks. He gives me a puzzled look as if trying to place me. I know that look. That's the *I've Seen You in a Movie Before But What Movie Was It?* look. I ignore it.

Without taking my eyes off Jacob, I answer. "My date's already here."

The host lets me through, and I head to Jacob's table, which is just big enough for two people and is tucked near the window.

The first thing I notice about Jacob is how attractive he is. Every aspect of his face seems to come together perfectly. There's a bit of stubble surrounding his jawline, but it's well-groomed and suits him. His medium-brown hair is short, but his most notable feature is his green eyes. They're captivating.

Juliet never told me how old he was, but he looks about my age, maybe a few years older. Observing this, I wonder briefly why he's on a date with me and not in a serious relationship.

As I approach the table, he smiles at me, and I note that his grin is not only friendly but is quite charming. Before I make it all the way there, he stands, moves to the other side of the table, and pulls out my chair for me.

As he sits back down in his own spot, I hold my hand out to him. "Siobhan Spencer," I introduce myself.

I can't seem to wipe the giant grin off my face. I can't believe I'm on a date. With a real guy. I feel like I should be more reluctant about this and less excited, but I'm just not.

"Jacob Bishop," he says as he shakes my hand with a firm grip. He has a purely American accent.

Damn, he's not from England.

As our hands touch, a spark flies between them. A literal spark. Not the butterflies-in-my-stomach kind of spark, but an honest-to-God shock conducts its way between our fingers.

"Oh, sorry," he apologizes with a grin as he shakes his hand in the air as if to rid it of electricity. "I'm feeling the sparks fly already," he teases.

He smiles up at me with beautiful eyes, and the fact that they're focused on me makes that spark come alive all over again.

CHAPTER FOUR

MENUS SIT in front of each of us. Jacob unlocks our eyes and opens his menu, staring down at it.

"Hmm... what sounds good?" he wonders aloud while I open my own menu.

I process the page in a second and realize that the food here isn't as expensive as I thought, although the ambiance is worth coming for. I'm pleased with the quiet conversations, soothing melodic string music, and delicious smells wafting from the kitchen. It calms my nerves considerably.

My eyes drift to the section labeled *Italian Entrées*, and after a moment's glance at the menu, I already know what I want.

"Gourmet raviolis," we say together, answering his rhetorical question. Our eyes lock again, and we each let out a small giggle.

"Gourmet raviolis it is," I say as our waitress reaches our table and greets us.

"Hello." She meets us with a smile. "My name is Alexis, and I'll be your server this evening."

Alexis sets two glasses in front of us and fills them with water, then leaves the pitcher between us. "Are you ready to order, or do you need more time?"

"I think we're ready," Jacob announces, handing her his menu.

"Fabulous. What would you like this evening?" Alexis asks, not taking her eyes off Jacob.

"Two orders of the gourmet raviolis, please," he says to her, and then he directs his next statement at me. "Would you like a drink?"

I take a moment to scan the beverage page. "A glass of red wine is fine," I answer, closing my menu and handing it to Alexis.

"I'll have the same," Jacob informs her.

"Okay," she says, jotting down our order. "We'll have that ready for you shortly. You two have a fantastic evening!" She turns and disappears.

A moment of awkward silence passes, and I'm the first to break it. "So, Juliet didn't really tell me anything about you. She said you two work together?" The statement comes out sounding like a question.

"Yeah," he confirms, leaning back and resting his entwined fingers on the tabletop. "I just started working at Watson's Gallery about a month ago. I've been helping Juliet organize exhibits."

I briefly wonder why he's not on a date with Juliet. I mean, she's a lot more attractive than I am, but then again, they're coworkers, and that'd be unprofessional.

Plus, she said he wasn't her type, though I'm not sure what that means. He's certainly attractive enough, and he seems kind so far.

"What did you do before you got a job at Watson's?" I ask curiously.

"I worked odd jobs while getting my degree, but I found this position through a friend of a friend, and I had to take it." He shrugs. "It's everything I wanted, and it's close to my apartment. Before this job, I was freelance writing on the side to earn a bit of extra income, but Watson's is paying me pretty well now, so I haven't been writing recently."

My face lights up, excited that we have something in common. "That is so awesome," I say with a bit too much enthusiasm. I tone down my voice. "I'm a freelance web designer."

I don't really want to talk about myself, though, so I gear the conversation back toward him. "What do you write about?"

"Tons of things." He lets out a bit of a laugh. "I've written for so many industries—finance, business, relationships, you name it."

"What type of publications have you written for?" I'm amazed at how even and confident my voice sounds even though my heart is fluttering on the inside. Is it my nerves, his smile, or my hunger?

"Mostly blogs, but I've had a few freelance writing gigs for magazines."

After a brief silence, I speak again. "Where did you grow up?"

I throw my series of inquiries at him, wanting to know more about this mysterious man. If he told me he grew up on a farm in the middle of nowhere, I might believe that he didn't have a television growing up.

"I'm a life-long New Yorker. And you?"

I shift uncomfortably in my chair. "I grew up in L.A."

"Oh," he says. "Why did you move to New York?"

I really don't want to talk about my childhood. "I visited the city when I was young, and I loved it here."

That's the truth. I don't have to tell him that I came here to film *Taking Reservations*.

"I always wanted to come back, so I came here to go to college and never left," I admit.

"Juliet didn't tell me much about you, either," he informs me. "Is there anything special I should know?"

My heart skips a beat. Oh, God. Does he know? Does he know I'm trying to hide my childhood so he won't judge me? Will he judge me for *that*?

My eyebrows come together. "I'm not three racoons in a trench coat if that's what you mean," I joke.

He laughs lightly, and I really enjoy the sound of it. "No, not like that at all. Do you travel much?"

Relief washes over me. "A bit when I was a kid, but not since I moved to New York. You?"

Jacob sits straighter in his chair. "After high school, I traveled around Europe for two years. I mostly stayed in London, but I visited France, Germany, and a few other countries."

I subconsciously fist-pump. God, yes. I did land an English man... sort of.

"What about you?" he asks.

"I've never been out of the country. There's not anything special about me." Because it's the only interesting thing to share, I blurt, "I haven't been on a date in two years."

Oh, God, why did I say that? That was embarrassing. He should not have to know how long it's been since I've had sex.

He smiles. "I haven't dated for a long time, either. I've been focusing on my career, you know?"

My heart rate begins to decrease back to normal. *So we're in the same boat.* Except his excuse seems valid, and I haven't dated in two years because in all honesty, I'm afraid of what the men I date will be like.

"Why did you agree to go out with me?" I wonder, and the question is out before I can stop myself.

He doesn't seem shocked by it. "Now that I'm settled in at a great gallery, I thought it wouldn't hurt to start dating again. Juliet was really persistent that we'd make a great couple when she heard I was single."

He smiles at me again, and my heart melts. So he wanted to date me because he has his career in check? That seems like a valid reason.

"Besides, I couldn't just say no to Juliet," he laughs. "You know what I mean."

"Absolutely," I agree. "I knew I couldn't get her off my back until I said I would do it."

I look down at my hands. "But I'm glad she persisted. I'm not disappointed."

My eyes move back to his, my head still down.

His hand reaches over to my chin, and he gently guides my head up. "I'm not disappointed, either."

He smiles, and for a moment, I feel lost. As I consider how I might never escape his eyes, Alexis returns with our meal, startling us. Jacob's hand recoils from my chin.

His elbow hits my water glass, and a shattering noise fills the restaurant as the glass topples over. Ice-cold water spills over my lap, and I yelp as I jump up, knocking my chair over behind me.

"Oh, God," Jacob cries, grabbing his napkin. "I'm so sorry."

I take the napkin he offered and pat my dress, but it doesn't help. "It's okay. It was an accident."

"We'll move you to another table," Alexis says quickly.

"Give me a minute?" I ask Jacob.

I hurry off to the bathroom and do my best to soak up the water with paper towels. The big splotch of water makes it look like I pissed myself, but if I position my purse just right over my shoulder, it's hardly noticeable.

My hands shake nervously, but I steady them at my sides. This date is going so well. I'm not going to let some spilled water ruin it.

I take a deep breath to steel my nerves, then leave the bathroom. I find my way over to Jacob, who's been moved to another corner of the restaurant.

Jacob's cheeks flame, and he presses a hand to the side of his head. "Did I completely embarrass myself?"

"No," I assure him, before smirking. "Not *completely*."

He sighs heavily and drops his hand. "Partially, I can live with."

I sneak a glance at my phone, which reads seven-twenty-two. The water situation falls to the back of my mind. Jacob officially wins the title of the longest date I've been on without the guy recognizing me. My heart flutters again as I sit down.

Jacob wears the most adorable grimace on his face. "You sure you're okay?"

Holy crap, this guy is charming, I tell myself, and I silently thank Juliet for setting us up.

"Absolutely. It's just ice water. No one got cut on the glass. Crisis averted."

Our food is already set in front of us. I pick up my fork and shove a ravioli in my mouth. I chew at in furiously. After a moment, I realize how ridiculous I must look, and I slow down. I let the ravioli sit in my mouth as I focus on its flavor and let it gratify my taste buds.

Jacob places one of his own raviolis in his mouth and lets out a groan of pleasure. He chews and swallows before announcing, "This food is heavenly."

Because I'm not sure what else to say to him, I continuously place food in my mouth so that I don't have to speak.

Jacob seems nervous after the water incident, because he doesn't say anything, either.

I'm not sure if this date is completely ruined, but I find myself wanting to salvage it. Halfway through my meal, I break the silence, and I manage to squeak out another question. "Do you have any brothers or sisters?"

He finishes chewing and answers. "I have one sister and one brother. You?"

"One sister. Do both of your siblings still live in New York?" I ask.

"No. Well, my sister just moved back after getting out of a long relationship. She lived in California for a few years. My brother is in Chicago."

"And your parents?"

"After they retired, they moved to Florida, so my family is kind of spread all over the place." He takes a bite of his food and then continues after he swallows. "What about your family?"

"They're all still in L.A. It's just my parents and my sister."

The conversation goes quiet again. I'm *really* nervous.

I'm still finishing the last few raviolis on my plate when he speaks. "All right, *Get to Know You* rapid-fire edition."

I sit straighter in my chair. "Sounds fair. You first."

"What's your birthday?" he asks.

"May twelfth. You?"

"January twenty-second."

"Medical history?" I wonder. "Any broken bones?"

"When I was two, I fell out of my highchair and had to

get stitches on my nose." He talks with confidence as he rubs his finger on the bottom of his nose. I'm amused. "When I was seven, I fell off the monkey bars at the park and broke a bone in my wrist. And when I was nineteen, I foolishly stubbed my toe on the edge of a chair and broke it."

I give a giggle. "Which one?" I ask when I swallow my last ravioli.

"The second toe on my right foot."

"Well, Mr. Bishop," I tease. "It seems that I know everything about you now. Your stubbed toe explains it all."

He smiles at me, entertained by my humor. "Yet I seem to know nothing about you, Ms. Siobhan Spencer."

I can't help but smile at him because of his charm, but a part of me wants to shy away at the same time.

"Did anything exciting happen during your child-hood?" he asks me, and my face falls.

Seeing this, his expression mirrors mine. "I'm sorry," he apologizes. "Did I say something wrong?"

I don't want to talk about my childhood, I answer in my head.

"No," I assure him, trying to put on an expression of approval, which I think I succeed at. "I just don't have any great stories like that to tell."

"Really?" He seems surprised. "No stitches or broken bones whatsoever?"

"Nope."

"No trips to the emergency room?"

"Nope."

"Well, you must have had one boring childhood," he teases with a smile.

"Yeah," I agree, and I try to come up with a joke to play along, but my mind can't seem to muster one. I simply smile back and take a sip of my wine.

The way he stares back at me tells me that this guy has nothing up his sleeve. Although my paranoia has been toying with me all night, I get the feeling that this is a guy I can trust.

I tilt my head back and chug the rest of my wine. He raises his eyebrows at me.

I raise my brows back at him. "I may not have had an exciting childhood, but no one stays the same forever."

"Indeed," he agrees, and he holds his wine glass up as if to toast and then puts his glass to his lips and tilts his own head back as he lets the wine rapidly flow down his throat.

We grin at each other dreamily. God, there's so much smiling going on tonight. I lose myself in his eyes as we continue talking about things that don't matter. I'm so captivated by him, and I can't seem to process anything he's saying for more than a few moments.

When our waitress returns and takes our plates, Jacob quickly orders dessert before she leaves. He lets me choose my own dessert, and I agree to whatever he's having.

Despite the small talk and the short time I've been with him, I know that Juliet hit this one right on the nose. Jacob and I share the same type of humor, and we're getting along very well. I'm actually enjoying myself, and I surprisingly no longer feel that first-date awkward nervousness in the air. This is already turning out to be my best blind date yet.

When the dessert arrives a few minutes later, Alexis places a piece of chocolate French silk pie in front of me. I take a bite, and it melts in my mouth. As I watch Jacob slowly put his own piece of pie to his lips, I wonder if this is what it would taste like to kiss him.

Would I melt like this? Would it be sweet? I don't know. I haven't kissed a guy in so long that I can't quite remember what kisses taste like.

We eat our pie slowly, taking longer to consume these small slices than it took to eat our entrées, and we simply talk. Who's my favorite actor? What's my favorite color? What's my favorite type of music?

"Fears," he states, highlighting our next subject. "Are you afraid of anything? The dark? Heights? Small, enclosed spaces? Spiders?"

"God, no," I reply. "No, no, no, and no."

I make a checkmark in the air for each item on the list. "I am fearless."

The questions go on, and as much as I'm trying to make my pie last as long as possible, it disappears before I know it. By the time I reach the last bite, it seems to have a stale, old texture to it. We must've been sitting here for over an hour.

When the check comes, he grabs it before I get the chance to play the check dance with him. Do people not do that anymore? God, I haven't dated in so long I don't know.

"I can pay for myself," I offer.

"I insist," he says kindly.

Jacob pays the bill, but I pull out some cash and leave a tip on the table.

I'm not ready for the night to end.

CHAPTER FIVE

WE EXIT the restaurant and stand awkwardly for a moment.

Jacob glances at his watch, and a shocked expression forms across his face. "Ten o'clock already. I really need to get home."

I'm stunned as well. I can't believe we were talking that long. The time seemed to fly, and I realize that we were sitting with our pies for quite some time. "Yeah, I have to get an early start tomorrow morning."

I don't want to leave yet. I'm really enjoying my time with him. "Let me walk you home," I offer.

"I'd love the company," he accepts as the corners of his mouth raise slightly.

I don't realize until several blocks later that it may sound like I'm trying to get in bed with him, but I hadn't meant it that way. He walks casually, like he isn't expecting anything from me, either.

We walk side by side as we continue the series of random questions, agreeing most of the time but arguing about other answers. It's strange how natural it all feels. Although Jacob freely answers my questions and we joke together, I know there are much deeper, more personal questions I want to ask. Even so, I hold back. I don't understand why I'm so afraid.

I watch him as we walk, and I notice my face is beginning to hurt. I haven't stopped grinning for hours. Taking note of this, I realize that I'm already falling for this guy. I quickly push that thought aside.

I don't even know him, I tell myself. Another voice emerges from the back of my mind and whispers, *But you still like him.* And just like that, my answer strikes, and I realize why I'm so afraid.

I don't want to get personal because I want him to like me for *me*. I want him to like me for the way I act, and I want him to fall in love with my charm, not judge me for any of the details that don't matter in a relationship. As I watch him speak, I understand what it's like to enjoy someone for who they really are, not what their past says about them. I'm not ready for him to learn about mine.

The walk doesn't seem long enough, even though his apartment is farther from the restaurant than mine is.

"Well, this is it," he says as he sticks his hands in his pockets and shrugs his shoulders up to his ears. He seems nervous, though I don't know why. He appeared so confident the rest of the night.

"I had a really great time tonight," I tell him.

"Me, too," he agrees as he charms me with a half-smile while looking down at me. Jacob is a lot taller than me, but he's comfortably taller with my heels on.

"Which one are you in?" I ask, gesturing toward the building and not yet wanting to leave.

"Apartment 202. Easy enough to remember." He bites his lip for a moment, stalling the conversation. "Would you possibly agree to another date?" His eyebrows rise with hopefulness.

I can't contain my excitement. "I'd love to!"

"Awesome," he lets out a breath and lowers his shoulders. "Are you busy Saturday?"

"I'm free all day," I say with a big grin that I can't seem to control. I feel sixteen all over again.

"Let's make a day out of it, then. How does ten in the morning sound?"

An entire day with Jacob? Count me in!

Almost immediately, I feel something within myself recoil. Do I really want to get close to a guy like this? Is it worth it?

But he doesn't know who you are! another voice screams in my head. That has to count for something.

"Sounds great." I pause for a moment. "Where?"

"I'll pick you up. Juliet already gave me your address. You know, for work emergencies."

We both stand silently for a minute, not wanting to take our eyes off each other. My eyes shift around his face, landing upon his lips, up to his eyes, and then back to his lips. His eyes are scanning my face in the same manner.

Jacob closes the distance between our bodies, and as he comes closer, I can't help but inhale his scent. My God, he smells glorious. Like a... Well, he smells like the damn-fine sexy man he is.

He's close enough that I can feel the warmth radiating off his body, and my head momentarily goes dizzy as I breathe in his magnificent aroma.

I see him watching my lips, and my heart races to keep up with the butterflies dancing around in my stomach. My head tilts up at him, my eyes locked on his lips, and my own lips quiver in anticipation.

Kiss me, I want to beg.

Somehow, he reads my mind. Jacob leans down, and our lips connect. Suddenly, an intense flame ignites in my abdomen, and the butterflies in my stomach begin dancing to a new tune—a wilder, more upbeat tempo.

Jacob's lips are as soft as they look, and to my surprise, he *does* taste as sweet as the French silk pie we had in the restaurant. Reaching up, I wrap my arms around his neck, and I let myself melt into him. He gently places his arms around me and pulls me in closer. My skin burns, particularly near the area where his lips are touching mine, and a strange, warming sensation finds its way between my thighs.

My God. This guy is turning me on.

I carefully entwine my fingers into his hair, and he does the same to me. I let out a soft moan and part my lips. His tongue moves inside my mouth, and this part of him tastes even sweeter than his lips. We press our bodies together.

Is a first date kiss supposed to be this passionate? I wonder.

It doesn't seem to matter the answer because I find myself responding to him in a way that makes me feel like I understand all of his intentions. It's like we both know just how far we're both willing to go.

He pulls away from me gently—and far too soon—with his eyes still closed. Letting out a breath, he opens them as a grin forms across his face.

Only then do I have a moment to fully process what just happened. *Did* that just happen? I can hardly believe it. A kiss like that isn't supposed to happen on a first date, is it?

"I really do have stuff to do tomorrow," he utters, and I know the passionate moment is over, even though my blood is still flaming with desire.

"I totally understand," I tell him, although I really didn't want to leave him. Now that I've tasted him, I want more.

"I'll see you on Saturday," he promises, and he leans down to give me one more peck before turning toward his apartment. I watch him leave, and before he enters the door to his building, he gives me a wave and a gentle smile. "Tell Juliet thanks for setting us up."

"I will," I promise.

Once he disappears, I turn to head back toward my own apartment. I'm beaming with satisfaction. Even in my heels, I give a skip of excitement. I can't place why I'm so happy. If anything, I should be more wary of things going so well. But for the first time in a long time, I don't want to push him away.

Juliet was certainly going to get a thank-you from me.

CHAPTER SIX

WHEN I ARRIVE HOME, Juliet is in the living room and has her painting supplies out. A large piece of plastic is spread across the floor under her, and an art easel with an unfinished painting stands on top of that. She holds a brush in her hand. I wonder if she's still awake so she can ask me about my date or if she has actually lost herself in her painting. I'm guessing it's the former.

When I walk through the door, her face immediately lights up, and she sets her brush down. "So, how'd it go? Did you like him?"

I certainly don't want to admit that Juliet was right, but I can't hide my pleasure. Trying to mask my exhilaration, I force the smile off my face. My muscles fight back at me, and the corners of my mouth quiver as my face flames.

"It was good." I shrug, trying to act indifferent.

Juliet sees straight through me.

"Good?" she asks, not believing my words. "Siobhan, you're glowing. You like him."

I can't fight my body anymore, and the grin escapes my grasp. "Yes, Juliet. Thank you."

"I told you," she boasts. "So, will there be a second date?"

I blush. "We're spending Saturday together."

She raises her eyebrows. "Luckily for you, I won't be home until late Saturday night, so you'll have the place to yourself for a while."

"What?" I squeak. "Where will you be?"

"I have a huge project I'm working on. I'll be at the gallery on Saturday."

I know what Juliet is doing, and I glare at her. "Doesn't Jacob have to help you with your project?"

"No. I'm going solo on this one."

I'm not sure if I believe her. I'm pretty certain she came up with this project just now.

"Well, I'm tired," I announce. I turn to my bedroom with tired eyes, but then I remember something. "Juliet, Jacob told me to tell you thanks for setting us up."

She grins at me, and I escape the room before she can start asking me details and making me describe our intimate kiss in detail.

In my room, I remove my heels and dig my toes into the soft carpet, enjoying the feeling of freedom on my feet. I slip off my dress, remove my contacts, and crawl into bed. Completely relaxed, I relive the kiss over and over, allowing the fluttering in my stomach to continue without repressing it until I fall asleep.

When I wake, I almost believe the previous night was a dream, but as my eyes fall upon my dress and heels strewn lazily on my floor, I realize it was real. My heart jumps, and my mind runs through the details of the date once again, trying to memorize Jacob's face and burn it into my memory.

Finally, I force myself to get up and shower, then I sit down at my computer and prepare to work. Instead of accomplishing anything, however, I end up losing track of time, realizing that I've been staring at the screen for nearly twenty minutes without making any progress.

My phone begins singing at me, making me jump. I have to get up and dig it out of my purse, which is across the room on my dresser. I look at the caller ID and see it's my sister, Mackenzie.

"Hello," I answer, and she screeches back in my ear. There are no words coming from her mouth, just an earth-shattering shriek of excitement. I pull the phone away from my face and stare at it, afraid it might be broken.

"Siobhan, I'm getting married!" she squeals.

I know what I would normally be feeling right now. If she had called me any other day, I would be cursing the universe for blessing my sister with breasts *and* a man. I wouldn't believe that my sister, who is four years younger than me, found a man before I did.

But today, I don't feel any of that. I put on a genuine smile and congratulate her. "Mackenzie, that's incredible!"

"I know," she squeals again.

I look at the clock. "It must be really early in L.A. How come you're calling me now? When did he propose?"

"Like ten minutes ago," she raves with full enthusiasm. "Derek proposed this morning before I could leave for work—it's our anniversary—and I'm too excited to go in to work today. I'm engaged! Siobhan, it was *so* romantic. He made me breakfast in bed and got down on his knee and everything!"

She shrieks in excitement.

"Congratulations," I tell her genuinely.

"I have tons of other people to call. Mom and I are going to look at dresses sometime this week, so I'll send you some pictures, but you have to *promise* not to share it with Derek. And just so you know, the wedding is going to be in December sometime. We want to get married before the end of the year."

That's fast, I think, though I don't say anything.

"Okay, thanks for calling me, Mackenzie," I say. I internally laugh at her for thinking I would show a picture of the dress to Derek. I hardly know the guy and only met him at Christmas last year when I went to visit my family in L.A.

"No problem," she says. "I'll talk to you later. Bye."

"Bye," I say and hang up.

I attempt to get back to work after Mackenzie's phone call, but it becomes increasingly difficult with the thoughts of a wedding in my mind. Without success, I put my work aside and let my feelings run free by updating my blog.

What is Love? I'd Really Like to Know

By Siobhan Spencer

Love. It's a word so full of emotion, yet people tend to abuse the term far too often. People throw it around like it's a basketball, tossing it to the floor, sharing it between others, and throwing it in the air. Is this fair to love? That's not how it was designed.

Then again, what do I know? I've never been in love before. Sure, I've shared intimate moments with men, but did I love them? No, I did not.

I'm clueless.

The thought of romance has been swimming in my mind since last night, which, I'll admit, was my first date in two years. Yes, I'm a loser. But that's not the point.

I'm not saying I'm in love by any means. After all, I just met the guy. Am I hoping this will go somewhere? Perhaps. So with this man's smile in my mind and the recent announcement of my sister's engagement, I wonder about love. What is love?

Is it the butterflies in your stomach? Is the burning sensation that races through your veins when you share a first kiss? Is it the fact that you can't get him out of your mind?

I don't have an honest answer.

Love... What is love? I'd really like to know.

I don't reread the post. When I blog, I try to keep my words honest without editing myself too much, and I write posts based on whatever's on my mind. I tend to get really great responses from my followers, too, which is one of the reasons I love blogging. My followers always come to me with even more advice, and it helps me understand my thoughts and issues better.

I place my cursor over the publish button. As I press down on my mouse, I wonder why I'm able to freely share my mind, unedited, with readers across the world, yet I tend to hide parts of myself when I come face-to-face with real people.

I'm not sure that's a question I want to know the answer to.

I press publish anyway.

When Juliet arrives home from work, she doesn't waste any time barging into my room, sitting on my bed, and beginning her inquisition. I can tell that she's been dying to get the details since last night, but since I escaped with my excuse of exhaustion and I didn't wake up before she went to work, this is her first opportunity.

"Dish," she commands. "Jacob was all smiles and bubbly today at work. What exactly happened last night?"

I swivel my computer chair around to look at her. "We just kissed," I tell her, trying once again to act casual without success. "It was no big deal."

"No big deal?" she squeaks. "Siobhan, I've never seen a smile that big on your face in all the years I've known you."

I suddenly realize that I *am* grinning as I replay the kiss in my mind.

"Well, he's a really good kisser," I admit.

"Did anything else happen?" Her voice is a bit higher than normal.

"No, Juliet. We just talked and he kissed me good-night. That's it."

She doesn't seem to believe me. "You're no fun." She frowns, and I can tell that she was hoping for a bit more flame to my story. "Well, you two obviously like each other."

"The date went well. We're spending time together again on Saturday." I stare down at my hands, once again trying to mask my smile.

"There's got to be more to it than that," she insists.

"It was a bit awkward at first," I admit, remembering how I didn't know what to say to him. "But after dessert arrived, we couldn't stop talking. I guess I'm just really comfortable around him."

She rises from my bed. "Well, you should be. You two make a great couple."

I wonder exactly how she knows this when she's never seen the two of us together.

"I hope you have a bit more to tell me next time." She winks as she leaves the room.

Later when I go to bed, I'm once again unable to put the daydreams about Saturday out of my mind.

Friday passes in a way that almost mirrors my Thursday, except that I head to yoga class in the morning. My nerves are still alive and well, but I try not to let them get to me. Today, I'm a bit more in tune with my body, and I let myself relax.

When I arrive home from my morning yoga session, I sit down at my computer, once again staring at it without touching the keyboard for several minutes. My mind is a bit more productive today but still not back to normal. Eventually, I dive into my work, trying desperately not to get sidetracked.

My attempts fail when the doorbell rings around two o'clock. I jump, surprised at the noise. I'm not expecting anyone. I walk to the door and open it. Staring back at me is a stunning bouquet of yellow roses. The delivery man behind them is looking down at a piece of paper and simply says, "Siobhan Spencer," although he struggles to pronounce my name properly.

"Yeah, that's me." My confusion bleeds through into the tone of my voice, and the man hands me the flowers. Looking up for the first time, his eyes scan my face, and his expression brightens.

"You look really familiar," he says.

"People tell me that all the time." I try to make my statement sound nonchalant. "I must have one of those faces."

"No," he says, shaking his pen at me as if the answer is on the tip of his tongue. "You're Celina, aren't you?"

God, I hate when people call me Celina.

"No," I reply. "I played her in a movie."

"Are you still acting?"

"No," I tell him. "I haven't acted since I was seven."

Letting him take this in, I turn back into the apartment with my flowers and close the door behind me. I know I was rude, but I've experienced this encounter far too many times to care.

I turn my attention to the beautiful bouquet in my hands. Attached to them is a hand-written note that reads:

Looking forward to our second date.
   -Jacob

The butterflies in my stomach dance as my heart flutters, and soon I feel the sensation throughout my whole body. I press the flowers to my nose and take a nice long whiff. They smell wonderful. I take in this moment because it's the first time that anyone has ever sent me flowers.

I head to the kitchen and find a vase under the sink. I return to my bedroom and place the yellow bouquet on my computer desk with the note facing me.

I beam. This guy really is incredible.

For the rest of the day, I'm unproductive because I can't stop stealing glances at the flowers. Right now, I'm cursing myself for never getting Jacob's number. I want to call him and thank him for the flowers.

When I'm ready for bed, I find it hard to sleep, unable to stop fantasizing about the day to come.

Finally, I drift off to sleep, and I dream of green eyes.

CHAPTER SEVEN

MY EYES SHOOT OPEN, and I can't see anything. For a moment, I'm disoriented, but after my eyes adjust to the darkness, I realize I'm still in my bedroom. I look at the clock. It's five-thirty in the morning.

I want to go back to sleep, but as I roll over and close my eyes, I find it challenging. I'm wide awake. Failing at my numerous attempts to fall back asleep, I push the covers away and crawl out of bed. I've been fighting my body for seventeen minutes now without success.

I have plenty of time on my hands, so I fire up my computer. Once on, I check my email, then scroll through social media. I check my blog comments and reply to people, and I'm very satisfied with the responses I've received about love. I'm a bit disappointed to find out that some of my readers don't believe in it, but the commenters who have truly experienced love greatly outweigh this negative feedback, and I become increasingly hopeful.

When I've exhausted all my duties online, I look at the clock again. It's six-forty-two. I went through that way too fast. Ten o'clock can't get here soon enough.

I close my laptop and make my way to the kitchen. As I'm pouring myself a bowl of cereal, Juliet exits her bedroom.

"You're up early," I tell her.

"So are you," she points out.

"Not really. I get up earlier than this three times per week to go to yoga."

"Couldn't sleep?" she asks.

"Not really."

Juliet enters the kitchen and reaches into the cupboard, pulling out a cereal bowl. She stares at me with that huge smile again. "Siobhan's got a date," she sings.

My cheeks flame. "Shut up."

"I read your blog post," she teases. "You really like him. It's obvious."

I roll my eyes at her. Ten o'clock really can't come any sooner.

I eat my cereal quickly so that I don't have to deal with Juliet's teasing for long. Once I'm done, I wash my bowl and head to the shower.

I take my sweet time, but when I get back to my bedroom, I'm shocked to see that it's only seven-oh-three. I feel as if some magical force is slowing down time just to fuck with me. I check my phone just to make sure the clock in my room isn't broken. Nope, it's still seven-oh-three.

I head over to my mirror, and I'm stunned when I see

myself. This girl looking back at me is happy. As I think about Jacob and my smile widens, I feel my face burning. I notice there's actually color to it and that my symmetrical dimples are now visible. I look good, and today, I don't criticize my reflection.

I dance around my room like a teenage girl, although there's no music to swing my hips to. Despite this, I let my body flail as I sing in my head. I can't hide how thrilled I am even though I'm in solitude. When I finish my happy dance, I catch one more glimpse of myself in the mirror. I am radiant.

I spend an hour experimenting with my hair, another good chunk of time on my makeup, and eternity picking out my outfit for the day.

When I'm done, my hair is piled atop my head in an elegant updo with my bangs framing my face. I put on my fanciest pair of jean shorts with a multi-colored flowing tank top to match. Since I'm not sure what we're doing and I hope it's casual, I finish off my ensemble with my light blue converse. My makeup is simple, just bright enough to add a natural glow to my face, and I'm satisfied with my casual date look.

I set out a fancier outfit so I can change quickly in case Jacob shows up in more elegant attire, but I'm hoping that I won't have to. I'm comfortable in what I'm in. I feel like *me*.

When I'm done preparing myself, I look at the clock again. Nine-oh-eight. I still have an hour. I head out into the living room and notice that Juliet is already gone. I'm not surprised.

Twiddling my thumbs, I turn on the TV to kill time, but I can't seem to pay attention to it. Instead, my eyes study the second hand as it ticks around the clock above the TV. As ten o'clock nears, I become even more nervous.

Once ten hits, I'm so excited that I leap from the couch and jump up and down in the privacy of my apartment. I'm anxious for him to get here, and when the doorbell rings at precisely ten-oh-three, my heart swoons. I know I'm acting like a teenage girl, but I don't care right now. I have a second date with Jacob Bishop.

I grab my purse, take a deep breath to calm my shaking body, and answer the door.

Jacob is dressed casually in a light grey t-shirt that displays his biceps, a pair of khaki shorts, and sneakers.

"Ready?" he asks.

"Ready," I say. I exit the apartment, closing and locking the door behind me.

As we walk down the hall, he gently places his hand around my waist, and with a small tug, he pulls me close, bends down, and kisses the side of my lips. I melt.

"Where are we going?" I ask, smiling up at him.

"It's a surprise."

When we make it to the base of the building, we exit into sunlight and clear skies. The air is a bit warm, but it's pleasant. Jacob waves down a taxi, and we climb in. He leans forward and tells the driver our destination, but I don't hear what he says. I don't care where he takes me right now. I'm just happy to be next him, so close that I can feel the warmth of his body on my skin. It's a comforting feeling.

Jacob leans back and looks me in the eyes, smiling. "Are you ready to have some fun?" he asks rhetorically.

"Yes," I reply anyway. I'm beyond excited to be sharing my Saturday with him, and I'm even more eager to get back to kissing him. The other night was simply thrilling, and I can't wait to share a moment like that with him again.

He grabs my hand and entwines his fingers through mine. "Good."

My stomach flutters, and seeing my approval, he pulls his hand from mine and puts his arm around me, pulling me in close to his chest. I can smell him again, and I secretly steal long inhales so that I can take in his scent. He smells wonderful.

After a few moments, I look up at him. "Thank you for the flowers."

"No problem." He grins.

Mentioning the flowers, it reminds me about asking for his phone number, and confidently, I do. We exchange phones and put our numbers in each other's phones. I hand his back. He fiddles with it for a moment before placing it back in his pocket. He then pulls me into him again, and I'm comfortable as my head rests on his shoulder.

A few seconds later, my phone buzzes, and I check it. It's a simple text from Jacob that says, *Hi*.

I narrow my eyes at him. He smiles back and laughs.

On the rest of the ride, we play the question game again, trying to really get to know and understand each other, and although I know we've been in the taxi for a while, the ride ends far too soon.

I haven't been watching where we were going, and when I look up, I realize that we've escaped the tall buildings. In front of us spans a vast lawn dotted with people, and I can see the water covering the landscape beyond the grass. But that's not the only thing I notice. Rising up from the lawn is a beautiful wheel that towers above all the people.

A Ferris wheel. He's taking me on a God-damn Ferris wheel ride. My mind silently fist-pumps.

"You said the other night that you weren't afraid of heights," he says, confirming that I'm okay with this.

"No," I tell him, not taking my eyes off the magnificent structure. "I'm not."

A Ferris wheel seems very romantic. I feel like the luckiest girl in the world right now.

We exit the taxi, and he pays the driver. Together, we cross the lawn and make our way to the giant wheel that rises above us.

Jacob hands the guy at the wheel some money, and in exchange, he receives a long string of tickets. He rips a few tickets off the string and returns them to the guy, and the Ferris wheel comes to a stop.

When we crawl into our seat, Jacob's arm returns to its rightful position around my shoulder. My body eases.

The Ferris wheel moves, and we're transported to the

top where it stops to let on more passengers. Up here, the view is exquisite. We're high in the air, and the people below us look like ants. The sun reflects off the water, as well as the brilliant skyscrapers, and the sky is clear blue, creating a picturesque scene.

I'm so caught up in the romance of the moment, with his arm around me and the beautiful city surrounding us, that I don't want to break the silence. Jacob, however, doesn't read my telepathic message.

"It's beautiful, isn't it?" he asks.

"Simply spectacular," I agree, and we share with each other our favorite aspects of the scenery.

I enjoy the way the sun gleams off the skyscrapers, and Jacob loves how far we can see the blue sky span.

The Ferris wheel begins to move again, and the soft swing of our cradle, coupled with the comfort I find in Jacob's embrace, soothes me. I don't want to get off this Ferris wheel anytime soon. It's serene here, and I don't want this moment to end.

After only rotating the wheel a few times, the guy controlling the ride stops it to let us off, but Jacob simply rips off more tickets and hands them to the guy. He lets us continue. We do this until all our tickets are gone.

"This is incredible," I say. "The city is so... artistic."

Jacob agrees, and our conversation moves toward our shared captivation in the city's architecture.

I'm a bit disappointed when we run out of tickets, but I don't want to have to pay for more, so we exit the ride. The Ferris wheel isn't the only exciting thing here, though.

There's a path that runs along the water with various vendors lined up on each side. Jacob grabs my hand, and together we explore the place.

My eyes first fall upon a cotton candy vendor, and I race up to the window.

"Cotton candy? Awesome." Jacob nods his head in approval.

"One cotton candy, please," I order at the window, and the young man, probably still in high school, grabs a stick from the pile and twirls it around the cotton candy machine until a sugar cloud forms.

Jacob reaches for his wallet.

"I've got this one," I stop him, and I pull out a small bill. Jacob doesn't argue with me, and I like that he lets me pay. It makes me like him even more.

Once we make our way from the vendor, I pull off a wad of cotton candy and place it in my mouth. It melts deliciously on my tongue, and it reminds me of the kiss Jacob and I shared the other night. God, I want to kiss him like that again. I offer him some, and he accepts with a smile.

I watch as he places his wad of cotton in his mouth, and I'm desperately wishing that I was that piece of cotton candy right now. I want to touch his lips and taste his tongue, but I don't get the chance.

Once we're finished and have licked our fingers clean, I throw the stick away in a nearby bin. When I look up, there's a photo booth staring back at me.

I don't have to ask Jacob if he wants a photo with me. I

simply walk up to the booth, and he follows. I let myself in first, and then I grab his shirt and pull him in after me. His eyes widen in surprise.

He closes the curtain behind us, and we giggle together as we plant a long, hard kiss on each other's lips. I'm transported to an entirely different place, floating above the city, higher than the Ferris wheel. His lips are so soft against mine, and the feeling I get within my chest as my heart rate increases leaves my body shaking. I'm completely captivated by this man.

We pull away from each other, and the kiss is over. I'm disappointed, but I know we didn't come into the photo booth to make out.

I feed a few dollars into the machine, and we choose the settings that we want. We have four shots, and I want to make them count.

I'm laughing, fully enjoying myself. "What poses should we do?"

"I don't know," he laughs back at me. The timer is already ticking for our first shot. "Say cheese," he orders as the flash goes off, and I grin along with him. My grin spreads so far across my face that my eyelids press together hard.

There are only a few seconds in between shots. "Silly faces!" I suggest, and I cross my eyes and puff out my cheeks as he scrunches his face up and sticks his tongue out. The flash goes off.

"Mustaches," I say as I place my pointer finger above

my upper lip, and he follows along, smiling into the camera. *Snap.* The camera captures our photo.

For the last one, I make it extra special, and just a moment before the camera flashes, I pull Jacob into me and plant a kiss on his lips. After the camera flashes, I pull away, beaming. He returns the smile.

We have to wait several minutes for our photos to develop, but we're soon presented with our snapshots.

I look them over, and I'm very pleased. When I get to the last one, I let out a loud laugh and throw my head back. In it, Jacob's eyes are wide with surprise, and it's clear I've caught him off-guard.

Since we received two copies of our photos, I hand one to him. He looks them over and chuckles, and then he reaches into his pocket and pulls out a pen. He flips over the photo strip and presses it against the wall of the photo booth and writes something on the back.

He hands it to me and takes the other one from my hand, depositing that one in his wallet. I look at the back of it.

I hope you had as much fun as I did!
 -Jacob

I smile up at him. "I did." I slip my photo strip into my purse for safe keeping.

When we're done exploring the area, we head back toward the street. He flags down another taxi.

"Where do you want to go now?" he asks as he kindly opens my door for me.

"Wherever you take me," I reply, and I let myself relax onto his chest, replaying the morning in my head as I again take in his scent.

I don't want to forget a single moment with him.

CHAPTER EIGHT

WHEN THE TAXI STOPS, we're in front of Central Park, and I'm glad we're here. Sometimes when I need a break from work or can't find inspiration for a blog post, I come here and walk the paths. Although it can get crowded, I find it serene.

Jacob and I climb out of the cab, and he hands the cab driver some cash. When we step into the daylight and warm, comfortable air, I take in a deep breath and feel the city touch my nose. I love this place, and I want to get away from the street and escape into the trees.

Jacob grabs my hand and leads me down the path. We walk at a leisurely pace. My heart is giddy with excitement as we stroll, but I don't let that show in the speed of my stride.

I lift my head and focus on the leaves above me. "Don't you just love it here?"

"It's a beautiful place," he agrees.

We walk in silence for a moment, taking in the bit of nature that the city allows us. I can tell by the look on his face and his long, calming breaths that he shares my love of Central Park.

When the silence ends, we go back to learning more about each other. Our next subject is books. I talk to him about my favorite novels, and he talks about the classics. My heart flutters when I realize that he's into literature. None of my previous boyfriends had cared.

We share our thoughts about the characters, plots, writing style, and so on until Jacob stops walking. I tear my eyes from him and follow his gaze. In front of us sits a beautifully decorated white horse-drawn carriage. The cab is empty, but there is a man tending to the horses.

"Do you like horses?" Jacob asks.

"Of course. Who doesn't?" I say.

Jacob releases my hand and greets the man, and I see him hand the guy some cash. My heart again swoons. He's taking me on a carriage ride. A goddamn carriage ride! No guy has ever taken me on a carriage ride.

He grips my hand again and guides me to the carriage. I climb into the cab, Jacob leading me up the steps. He trails behind me, and after the carriage driver takes a moment to situate himself, we're off.

I'm too stunned by the romantic gesture to speak. I mean, I've never even been on a carriage ride before, let alone with a guy, and I almost feel like I'm riding into my own fairytale. I'm Cinderella, and Jacob is my Prince Charming. I can't help but smile as he again pulls me into him. Suddenly, every woman around us is dressed in a stunning ball gown, and the men wear suits to match the Prince Charming look.

Jacob continues our conversation as if the carriage ride is nothing, and I'm pulled from my daydream of elaborate ball gowns. The carriage ride ends far too soon, and Jacob exits, helping me down with the support of his hand.

For a moment, I feel woozy. The step down from the carriage is farther than I anticipate, and I trip into him as my foot comes down onto the pavement. He catches me in his arms, and I get a good whiff of his scent again.

I blush, and I'm not sure if it's out of embarrassment—I'm not usually so clumsy—or if it's because of how his scent is turning me on.

"I'm sorry," I say, involuntarily biting my lip.

"No worries," he says as he takes my hand.

We continue on the path. I feel a bit better that he was able to shake off my embarrassing moment without much thought. I guess I was expecting him to make a joke at my expense or something, but he didn't.

I take in each moment with my breath, memorizing the city noises around me, the way the warm air feels on my skin, and each movement that Jacob makes next to me.

As we round a bend, I see a beautiful white structure rising above the pavement and hovering over the water. Ahead of us sits one of the most picturesque places in the city. I've been to this bridge before. It's the one you see often in movies. The first time I was here, we were filming *Taking Reservations*.

It's a truly magnificent sight, with the trees surrounding the water as they reflect off the glassy surface. We stop along the bridge and look out over the water. It's beautiful and green here, and my heart is full.

Together, we marvel at the scenery, and the conversation has switched from literature to our favorite pastimes. I tell Jacob about my web design, how I enjoy my yoga classes, and how Juliet and I go out dancing frequently. I talk to him about my blog, telling him how I use my blog as journal entries and that I love the way that people respond to me, giving me advice and sharing their own thoughts.

Listening to Jacob talk about his pastimes is more interesting to me than talking about my own hobbies, though. I'm intrigued as he tells me about how he loves photography. He takes out his phone to illustrate and places me against the side of the bridge.

"You stand here," he says as guides me to my proper position.

"Okay," I comply with laughter, fully enjoying myself.

Backing up, he holds up his phone and tweaks a few of the settings. I'm grinning, though he doesn't tell me to. I don't think I could stop if he asked me to be serious. I'm having far too much fun.

"Say cheese," he commands as he snaps a photo of me and my grin, the background gorgeous behind me.

When he returns, he shows me the picture, and I'm stunned at how beautiful I look. He gestures at different aspects of the picture, explaining the lighting and how different points balance out the photo. This guy isn't a painter like Juliet; his love of art lies in photography.

When it seems like we've covered every path in the park, it's already five o'clock. We reach an exit, and Jacob looks down at his watch. "Want to get something to eat?" he asks, and I realize that I haven't eaten anything since the cotton candy.

"I'm starving!" I agree, and instead of leading me to a cab, he takes my hand and walks down the street.

"Have any preference?"

"No," I answer. Right now, I don't really care what I'm eating as long as I'm eating it with him.

We walk another few blocks, and then he stops at a small pizzeria and opens the door for me. We enter, and the delicious scent of food hits my nostrils. The host leads us to a small two-person table and hands us our menus, taking our drink orders before he disappears.

"A pizza to share?" Jacob asks.

"Sounds great to me! How do you like pepperoni and sausage?" I ask.

Jacob's nose turns up. "I'm not too keen on the sausage," he tells me, and we compromise by agreeing on stuffed-crust pepperoni.

We know what we want before our drinks arrive, and we order our meal. Our conversation continues, and we talk mostly about the little things in life instead of divulging the larger details. We talk briefly about sports, and then the conversation turns to our favorite movies. By the time our pizza arrives, we're discussing our favorite restaurants in town. I'm beyond pleased that we haven't run out of things to talk about even though we've spent the entire day together.

My eyes widen as our waiter places our pizza in front of us. It's enormous and is cut into twelve pieces.

"I'm not going to be able to eat all this," I say, and Jacob laughs at me.

"That's okay, I'll eat your share," he tells me. I'm pretty sure he's joking.

I grab a piece and take a bite. The pizza is warm, fresh, and cheesy, and I'm not sure I've ever tasted anything so delicious.

I take a bite before Jacob does, and with a string of cheese running between my mouth and my pizza, he catches me off-guard.

"I really like you," he admits, and I stop mid-bite. My heart rate speeds, and the butterflies in my stomach come to life. He likes me. *He* likes me. He likes *me*.

He likes me for the way I act around him, not for the way I act on screen. He likes me for the time we've spent together, not for what he's seen of me in movies. He likes me because he enjoys my company, not because he thinks I'm rich or can make him famous. He likes me for *me*.

The concept is so foreign to me that I'm not sure how to react.

I finish chewing my piece of pizza and swallow. "I *really* like you, too," I confess, and he grins before taking a bite of his own pizza.

The pizza is too good to get any words in between

bites, so we simply shovel it into our mouths and cease our conversation. When I reach the end of my piece to the stuffed crust part, I let out a moan of pleasure. I take another piece.

Before I know it, I've eaten four slices of pizza. My stomach is about to burst. I force the last few bites of my fourth piece into my mouth.

"That was delicious!" I exclaim when I'm done, but Jacob still isn't finished. He nods his head in agreement mid-bite.

When he finishes and leans back in his chair, hands on his stomach the same way mine sit, there are two pieces left. "We'll each take one home," he offers, and he gestures to our waiter. "The check and two boxes to go, please."

We stare at each other dreamily until our waiter returns. Jacob once again grabs for the check before I get a chance, so I instead shovel a piece of pizza into each box. Then I throw a few dollars on the table as a tip.

We leave our table and pay our bill at the front, and then we walk hand-in-hand out of the restaurant.

CHAPTER NINE

WE STROLL LEISURELY, neither of us wanting the date to end. I'm surprised when Jacob's pace slows and he turns to another door in a nearby structure. He opens it and guides me into the building.

"Where are we?" I ask, but I realize where we are before he can answer. Well, not *exactly* where we are. I haven't been here before, but the white walls that span the vast room tell me we're in an art gallery. There's a front desk off to the left, and a man in a tight black sweater, blue scarf, and jelled hair sits behind it.

"We're about to close," the receptionist informs us.

"That's okay," Jacob says. "We won't be long."

The receptionist allows us through, and instead of exploring the gallery, Jacob leads me back to a single photograph.

A few people roam around, admiring the artwork, but

for the most part, the gallery is empty. I'm not used to this since I only go to galleries during receptions with Juliet, but I find this emptiness quite tranquil.

As I gaze around the room, I notice all the hanging works of art are of nighttime photography, all lit up by various parts of the city.

"Wow, they're so beautiful," I marvel.

"The exhibit is called *Nightlife*, and it's meant to represent the city at night. Different photographers around the city submitted their photos, and the best ones got in. I wanted to show you mine." Just then, he comes to a halt. I nearly trip over him because I'm paying attention to the photos instead of his pace.

There on the wall sits a gorgeous photo of a Ferris wheel lit up at night.

"Is that...?" My voice trails off.

"Yep," he answers. "That's the one we rode today."

"My God, you're talented." I don't give the compliment just to flatter him. I honestly mean it.

The photo is taken from the bottom looking up, and it cuts out about a third of the wheel, but the way the photo is balanced against the night sky, coupled with the crisp beauty of the lights, is enchanting. I can't tear my eyes off of it.

"I never thought I'd have my work in art galleries—let alone be working in one," Jacob admits.

I furrow my brow. "What did you want to do instead?"

"This. Art." Jacob gestures around the gallery, but his

gaze settles on his own photograph. "I never thought it was possible, though. For the longest time, I didn't know what I wanted to do. That's why I traveled so much. It's like I was trying to find an answer, but the answer was inside of me all along. I just... needed to listen to it."

"I'm glad you found your calling," I tell him. "You're a fantastic photographer."

Jacob blushes a little. "What about you? Did you always know what you wanted to do?"

"I always knew I loved art," I say. "But I was never a painter like Juliet. I really loved books and film, but I found I enjoyed *listening* to other people's stories, rather than telling my own. There's just so much beauty in other people's art."

I realize that's why I fell in love with acting. I've always loved bringing other people's artistic vision to life.

I begin walking slowly, eyeing the sensational photographs. "I think that's why I love web design so much. I get to create something, but I also get to be a part of something bigger. I get to help all these creative people build brands and make an impact. It's really special working with clients who are passionate about what they're putting out into the world."

"Who are your favorite clients to work for?" he wonders.

"I love working with small businesses—artists especially," I say. "If I can help people get their work online, it means more people get to enjoy their art."

"I don't think most people think that way. It seems

most people are just looking for a paycheck, but you really care about what you do."

I shrug. "The world wouldn't be the same without art. It's important, and not enough people recognize that."

Jacob keeps his eyes on me. "No, they don't."

"So, what's next for you?" I ask. "It seems you're living the dream, working in an art gallery and having your photos on display."

Jacob gives a light laugh. "I am, but I want to keep dreaming bigger. I want to connect with people on a deeper level. I want my photos to tell a story—maybe be on a billboard or something."

"A billboard would certainly be bigger." I smirk.

Jacob chuckles at my joke. "What about you? What are your big plans for the future?"

I press my lips together. "I want to keep making art."

"What kind of art?" he wonders. "If there were no limitations to what you could achieve, what would you want?"

I shake my head. "I don't feel like I have to dream bigger. I'm comfortable where I'm at."

Jacob arches an eyebrow. "Comfortable because you're happy, or comfortable because it's safe?"

His words stop me in my tracks, and I contemplate his question. I'm not sure of the answer, so I don't say anything.

My silence is an answer of its own.

"Maybe you just haven't found the right story to tell," Jacob offers softly.

I'm not sure what to think. I *like* my life, but I'm also

intrigued by Jacob's desire to dream bigger. I'm not sure what that would look like for me, though.

I pace back toward his photo. "Thank you for bringing me here."

He gives me a charming smile. "I'm glad you like it."

I take several more minutes to admire his photograph, really letting the colors captivate me. Soon, however, we're told that the gallery is closing, and we're forced to leave.

Together, we exit the building and continue walking, Jacob leading the way. I'm not paying any attention to where we're going, but we spend a long time walking. When I finally become aware of my surroundings, I realize we're in my neighborhood. Before I know it, we've arrived at my apartment complex. I don't want him to leave.

I twist my hands nervously. "Do you want to see some of Juliet's paintings? They're in the apartment. She's really quite good."

Jacob shrugs, though an eager smile crosses his face. "Sure."

We enter my apartment, and I set my box of pizza on the counter before leading him to Juliet's canvasses, showing off her talent. He studies the paintings, one hand on his mouth and the other supporting his elbow. He has a look in his eyes that Juliet gets every time she inspects a piece of art.

"It's beautiful." He raises his eyebrows, and I know he's impressed, but his focus doesn't last long.

Instead, he begins studying me. I shyly meet his stare.

His eyes roam downward to my lips, and I find myself drinking him in. Desire flashes in his eyes, and my breath catches. I realize he may not have been talking about the beauty of the painting.

"Yeah," I say breathlessly, admiring the green of his eyes. "It's beautiful."

I want him. *Badly.*

It's like he can read my mind again. In one swift motion, he closes the distance between us and presses his lips to mine. Within a single moment, I'm entangled in him. My legs wrap around his waist, until I'm no longer touching the floor.

He turns with me still clinging to him and takes a few steps forward until my ass touches the countertop of the breakfast bar. I run my hands all over his body to every part of it I can reach.

His arms wrap around me, and he gently slides them under my shirt and runs his hands across my back. I tremble, and a fire rises inside my body that makes my head spin.

I'm suddenly brave, and I pull away from him so I can jump down from the counter. With my new-found confidence, I take his hand and lead him into my bedroom. I stop in the middle of my room and kiss him lightly. Then I back up, and he follows until the back of my knees hit my mattress. I don't have to say a word for him to meet my desires, and together, we tumble onto my bed.

Jacob's body moves in sync with mine as passion surges

between us. I've never wanted anyone as desperately as I want him. He kisses me with fervor, and then his lips trail downward as my back arches off the bed.

He pulls away from me for a moment to remove his shirt. Desperate longing overcomes me, and I realize I crave is touch.

I reach for his waistband, and he smirks. His lips return to mine, and they never leave as he slowly glides my pants down my legs. My hands tangle in his hair as his hands roam over my breasts, then across the rest of my body.

I pant breathlessly as he kisses my collarbone, his warm breath tickling my skin. Neither of us speak as he pulls away and digs into his wallet for a condom. He places it in my hands, trusting me as I guide it over his length. Infatuation fills his eyes, and his whole body quivers in anticipation. Then he positions himself over me.

I gasp as he fills me up, thrusting into me and igniting a passion I've never experienced before. The chemistry between us is undeniable. I breathe a blissful sigh as he makes love to me as if our bodies were made to fit together.

His fingers trail downward, and he works my body until passion swells inside of me and we spiral into an earth-shattering orgasm together.

Over an hour later, there isn't a part of my body he hasn't touched—nor a moment when I don't feel *wanted*.

We fall onto the bed panting. Jacob pulls me close to his chest and kisses the top of my head.

"You're amazing, Siobhan," he whispers.

My heart flip-flops in response to my name coming off his tongue. I love the sound of his voice.

"Not as amazing as you," I sigh.

In that moment, I decide that there no better place than in his arms.

When I wake, Jacob is gone, and so are his clothes. I have to briefly confirm the details of last night to make sure that I wasn't dreaming the whole thing. Yes, I'm naked. Yes, I have sex hair. Yes, his used condom is lying in my trash can.

I had sex last night. I. Had. Sex. Last. Night.

I repeat this several times in my head before it really sinks in, and when it does, the grin that forms across my face has enough energy in it to light all of New York State.

But where is Jacob? I get out of bed and wrap my bathrobe around me, which is hanging on my closet door. On my computer screen sits two sticky notes with the same on-going message that reads:

I'm sorry, I didn't want to wake you, but I had to get back home. Please call me and let me know when I can see you again.

-Love, Jacob

Love!? Love, Jacob.

My heart flutters with excitement, and I feel like a

sixteen-year-old girl again. Finally, I've found someone that makes my heart long for him and swoon for him, and it's a thrilling sensation.

I read the note again. *Love, Jacob.*

Yes, I think I do.

CHAPTER TEN

What Is Love? I Think I Know

By Siobhan Spencer

A few days ago, I wrote that I would like to know what love is. Some of you responded saying you don't believe that love exists, that it is a delusion created by the hopeless romantics. Other commenters shared what they believe love is based on their own relationships.

First of all, I want to say thank you all for sharing your thoughts. Second, I want you all to know that I believe I've discovered what it is.

I don't want to say that I've never believed in love. I've certainly seen it before in couples I've known. It seems like all the members of my family are in love, and I can see it in their eyes. I see it in the way my sister Mackenzie stares at her fiancé, Derek. When I met him for the first time last Christmas, I knew she was smitten by him, and now they're getting married! I see it in my parents' eyes and the way they interact with each other. I've never heard them fight, and they're always treating each other with respect, even after thirty years of marriage.

So I guess what I'm saying is that I've always believed in love, but I wasn't always sure that I would find it. Today, as nervous as hell as I am to admit it, I feel like I can say that I've discovered love.

Is it the taste of his kiss? Is it the ache I feel in my chest when he's gone (believe me, I feel it!)? Or is it something that goes deeper than the physiological changes I feel when I think about him or when he's around or when— God, yes—he touches me?

I think I have an answer. My sort of love is one of desire, passion, and connection. It is an undeniable feeling of happiness and pleasure. It is a phenomenon that I cannot put into words.

Although I cannot give you a definition for love, I can tell you that I think I've found it.

MY HANDS TREMBLE as I type. I think it's out of exhilaration of my memories with Jacob, but I'm not entirely sure. Sometimes I have a tough time understanding what my body is trying to say, and now is one of those moments. How does this guy that I've spent so little time with have such an effect on me?

I hit publish, my heart racing. I just shared my deepest, most inner thoughts with the entire world, and I don't care. I know Juliet is going to race to my blog the first chance she gets to see what new things I have to say. I'm not sure if Jacob will research my website and read my words, but I don't mind if he does. I don't care that my followers are about to find out that I recently made love. I want the world to know I've found love.

As I think about Jacob researching my blog to check it out, I realize the time has come to reveal the secret of my childhood. He's bound to find out sooner than later, and I want him to find out from me, not from a Google search.

I don't want to tell him over the phone, so I decide to schedule our next date as soon as possible so I can tell him then. I don't want to hide anything from him, and I don't want him to feel like I betrayed him by not telling him. I'm ready to completely share myself with him, and that includes my past.

It's still early, but I find his number in my contacts and call him. My heart flutters when he answers.

"Hey," he greets. "Did you sleep well?"

"Fabulous," I answer. "When can I see you again?" I

try to keep my voice even, but it wavers a bit as I ask the question.

"I'm busy tomorrow, so how about we meet up Tuesday night?"

I'm more than happy to agree. I'm so thrilled that I don't even bother to ask what he's busy doing. I get to see him Tuesday night, and that's all that matters.

"I'm kind of busy right now," he says. "Do you mind if I call you later?"

"Not at all. I'll talk to you soon."

We hang up. I'm disappointed our conversation is over, but I'm ecstatic about Tuesday night. I hold my phone to my chest as I stare into the distance, replaying every detail of last night. My God, that was magical.

It's Sunday, and although I can work whenever I want, I try to leave the weekends open so I can take a break from work, so I quickly find myself at a loss of what to do. I'm too focused on Jacob right now.

As I think about him, my computer screen stares back at me, and I'm suddenly reminded that he's a writer. He said he's written for blogs before, and I'm instantly intrigued. I want to find some of his articles. I think if I can, I might gain some more insight into him. I'm not sure what exactly possesses me to start researching him, but I'm typing his name into the Google search bar before I can stop myself.

I shouldn't have been so naïve to think that one of his articles would show up on the first page. He has a fairly common name, and numerous other search results mask his. I flip through a few pages, but I don't find anything.

I begin searching social media. There are more results than I expect, so I narrow my search further, focusing on his location, place of employment, and age. After a while of searching, I finally see his face staring back at me. I click on his profile.

His profile picture is nice, just a simple photo of his face, but it looks professional, and his smile is to die for. Since I'm already on his page, I send him a friend request.

I continue my mission, and click on the About tab. There under Contact Information is exactly what I'm looking for. There's a link to a website, and I click on it.

This website is a simple one. *And in desperate need of a makeover*, I think as the web designer within me analyzes it. I catch myself leaning back in my chair, my elbow rested on my opposing hand, and my fingers to my chin. I quickly straighten up. I'm just as bad as Jacob and Juliet when it comes to admiring art.

His website advertises his writing services, and it has a welcome message, his rates, his specialties, his contact information, and—what I'm searching for—links to sample articles. There's also a professional portrait of him on the sidebar, and I stare at the photo for a bit, trying to memorize his face.

My heart begins to race again, but I manage to tear my gaze from his eyes and head to his sample page.

I begin clicking through the links. The first one is on finance, and I skim the article before closing the tab. The second link leads me to a blog about relationships, and I'm instantly intrigued by the title, "8 Ways to Please a Woman."

Jacob's professional photo, along with byline, sits under the title, and I begin reading. He doesn't divulge any details about how he knows all this, but he goes on to talk about how to spice up the romance, and he even gives sex tips.

Holy crap. Is this how he knows how to please me so well, both on our date and while making love?

I finish the article and return to his page of samples. I click on the next link, and the title takes me aback. My palms begin sweating, and my heart races.

My world comes crashing down.

CHAPTER ELEVEN

THE TITLE READS, "Child Stars: Then and Now." I want to refrain myself from clicking through the slide show, but I can't. There's a fire raging through me, and it's not one of desire this time. It's full of betrayal. I'm so confused.

Am I in it? Does he know me? It makes my blood flame as I consider the possibilities. My hands quake intensely as I press my mouse, making my way through the slideshow.

I'm a bit relieved when I reach the end of it and I haven't found my own face staring back at me, but I'm upset nonetheless. He knows about child stars. How could he *not* know who I am?

I take my research further, clicking on every sample link on his page, and my heart shatters when I find a new link. The headline says, "10 Things We Can Learn From Elizabeth River's Love Life."

Elizabeth River. As in the woman I costarred with in *Taking Reservations*.

I shoot out of my chair and begin pacing around the room. How could I be so stupid?

My eyes fall upon the vase of roses he gave me. Before I know what I'm doing, I grab the vase and heave them full force into my garbage can. Even in the moment, I know I'm overreacting, but everything within my gut is telling me that Jacob lied. The vase shatters, and then the room goes dead silent. I sink to the bed, staring blankly at the wall.

I can't explain why I do any of this. Fear grips me, and the betrayal burrows deep into my soul. I'm positive that he knows who I am. My God, this guy really knows how to put on a poker face. He really had me going.

I thought I could trust this man, but all that trust I recently put in him recoils at the speed of light, forming a black hole in my chest. What does that mean for our relationship? My chest aches, and a tension headache quickly forms. Jacob wrote this article about my costar. How can he not know who I am?

The web page stares back at me, taunting me. Shouldn't I have known this was too good to be true? I didn't even want to date him in the first place. Why did I rush it? Why am I such an idiot?

With my discovery of these two articles, it becomes pretty damn clear that he's writing a story on me. I'm crushed. I thought he liked me. Does he even care, or is he just trying to get a good story out of me?

People have written my words in articles before without my consent, and I still get journalists contacting me to ask me questions about my life today. Everyone seems to want to know what childhood actors have done with their lives, and I'm one of their biggest targets. Jacob is just another one of these people who wants nothing but page views out of me.

God, all those questions—about what I like, what I dislike, what I do, what my hobbies are—they're all things that someone would ask if they're trying to write a story on me.

I can see the article now, and my imagination puts the photo that he took of me in Central Park under the headline. I envision his article going something like this:

Siobhan Spencer: Childhood Star All Grown Up

By Jacob Bishop

Siobhan Spencer was once a beloved young actress that captivated the nation with her roles in Celina the Detective *and* Taking Reservations. *After her last film,* Beyond the Meadow, *Siobhan took a break from acting at age seven, never to return.*

But the nation still wants to know: Where is Siobhan Spencer now?

Today, Siobhan lives in a small New York City apart-ment with her roommate Juliet, who is much prettier and more successful than Siobhan. Siobhan hasn't dated in nearly two years and hasn't had sex in just as long, which is just plain sad when it comes to any woman, but it's a particularly troubling idea when you consider a former celebrity. Shouldn't a woman like this have men on her all the time? You'd think so, but that's simply not the case.

Love has little merit in her life; after all, she doesn't actively seek it but rather avoids it altogether. Instead, she closes herself off from the world and sits in her home designing web pages. She rarely gets out unless Juliet takes her with her.

What else do we know about Siobhan now? Today, she is a freelancer who finds solace in literature and in stuffing her face with pizza. Her preference: pepperoni and sausage. Perhaps the only good thing about her is the fact that she enjoys the view of the city atop a glorious Ferris wheel.

While Siobhan freely shares her feelings with the world on her blog, she has a hard time showing what she's feeling in real life.

Is this the kind of girl you want your daughters to look up to? Perhaps not. Siobhan gave up her dreams of acting when she was young, and she was never able to regain her strength and become successful in any aspect of her life...

I expect the article to go on longer than that, but I can't continue thinking about it. A feeling of emptiness wells inside my body, and my lungs constrict, compressing my heart and leaving it to lay in a million tiny pieces. These are the honest words that someone would say regarding a celebrity like me. I just know it, and I believe they're all true.

I fall to the bed and lay there for a long time, but I'm not able to gauge exactly how long. I can't seem to make my muscles work, as if this realization blocked my body's ability to move. I'm frozen in place, curled up in a ball, completely paralyzed.

When I regain enough strength to move, all I can do is pull the covers over me. I don't move for several hours, and the tightness in my chest never eases.

I can hear Juliet moving around in the kitchen as she prepares lunch for herself, and I'm thankful she doesn't take the initiative to come and talk to me. I'm shocked because I would have thought she'd take the first opportunity she got to begin questioning me about last night, but my door is shut, and I'm quiet. Perhaps she doesn't know I'm even home, or maybe she thinks Jacob is still in my bed. Whatever the reason, she doesn't bother me.

I stare at the ceiling for a while, and when I'm ready, I

get out of bed and sit down at my computer. I promptly delete my previous post. Then at my blog's dashboard, I open a new post template, and I begin typing.

CHAPTER TWELVE

Why I Hate People Who Write About Celebrities: A Former Celebrity's Perspective

By Siobhan Spencer

Most people know who I am. If they don't recognize my name, they'll recognize my face. If they can't place either, you just say the name of one of the movies I was in, and the connection instantly clicks.

But there are a few things I've learned about being a former celebrity throughout the years. First is the fact that people never stop recognizing you. Second, no one ever wants to stop telling your story. I can't count the number of times someone has contacted me in my adult life to ask for my most recent pictures, get a quote from me to put in their article, or ask me if I'm still acting. People want to know this shit, but it's hardly important.

When people start digging into my past and want to connect that with who I am now—a person who is twenty years older than the little girl they're trying to portray—it hits a nerve, and it hits it pretty damn hard.

If you just looked at my blog, you would know where I am today, and you wouldn't have to contact me about it. I do have a goddamn FAQ page. Why in the hell do you even care? All I did was act in a movie. Why not interview someone who actually matters?

I have a problem with this, and I'll give you a few pretty damn good reasons.

It's an Invasion of Privacy

Yes, celebrities do put themselves out there for everyone to see, but more often than not, it's in a professional manner. If a celebrity wants to share what time their scheduled bowl movements are, that is totally fine, but if they don't freely share that information, people shouldn't push them to answer it, especially when no one gives a fuck about the subject until they release the headline.

Bottom line: people who write about celebrities don't ever ask about the things that actually matter. Instead, they focus on the tiniest details about their lives, and getting that intimate is just fucking annoying. A celebrity shouldn't have to divulge what they had for breakfast, what type of underwear they're wearing, or—heaven forbid—who they're dating.

I won't even go into the sick details on how these writers gather this private information.

They're Fucking Mean

Celebrities are real people. They have feelings just like everyone else, but when you pick on them and bully them, it's not like it is for the rest of the world. Instead of a few people telling them how worthless, ugly, and imperfect they are, the entire nation gangs up against them and reiterates the same crude comments a million times.

When I was a teen, one of my friends searched my name online. When she found my bio, she thought it was so awesome that she shared it with me. I became intrigued, so I searched my name myself. What I found was awful. Not only were people criticizing me for leaving acting, but when a photo of my awkward teen years surfaced, they made fun of the way I looked, and said I was no longer celebrity material. For the longest time, I couldn't look myself in the mirror, afraid all those horrible comments would come back to haunt me.

Hell, let's be honest. I still can't look myself in the mirror.

They're Liars

People who write about celebrities lie. They lie all the time. Whether they do it on purpose or not, they always seem to get the facts wrong. Believe me, you can never trust what you read online or in magazines when it comes to a celebrity's personal life. Yes, I have experienced this, and it bites into a person's emotions deeply when the nation gangs up on them for something they didn't do or say, and these writers don't give a damn. All they care about is the amount of page views and comments they get.

This occurs in several ways:
1. They twist the words celebrities say or take them out of context just to make a great headline.
2. They misinterpret quotes, not taking into account body language or sarcasm.
3. They make shit up.

They're Untrustworthy

You know when people ask you a question, giving you their solemn word that they won't tell anyone what you said? Did this person ever divulge your words to the entire world? When I was just seven, they did this to me, and I quickly learned that people who write about celebrities are not to be trusted. No, I will not divulge the details, because frankly, you shouldn't really give a shit.

Needless to say, if you're a celebrity, you quickly learn that you don't talk to people with cameras or notepads because they are bound to stab you in the back. You cannot trust them.

They Have No Tact Whatsoever

Honestly, the way they shove microphones, cameras, and emails in your face is simply untactful. How about the time when I was just five and journalists were questioning me at the opening of Taking Reservations? *Do you know what they asked me? They didn't ask how I liked filming the movie, what I thought of traveling to New York City, or what it was like for my character. No, the question that they focused on was what I thought of Elizabeth River's latest sex scandal. My God, people. This is not something you ask a five-year-old. I didn't even know what they meant at the time!*

I hope you understand why you should never trust articles written about celebrities. These writers initiate a conversation that will bring a nation together to tear down one person's spirit. Perhaps now you understand why I'm so fucking afraid to let anyone in and terribly frightened to love a man.

I DON'T REREAD the post because I don't want to edit my words in any way. I want my passion and my anger to show through. I grit my teeth, and I hit publish.

CHAPTER THIRTEEN

ALTHOUGH IT'S ONLY about one o'clock, I wrap myself back in my blanket. My entire body is tense. The blanket doesn't seem to help my muscles relax, but it keeps me warm. My mind races with thoughts, wondering why Jacob would sleep with me, what exactly his motivations are, and what else he lied to me about. My thoughts bounce around in my head, but eventually, I drift off to sleep, and I'm out for hours.

When I wake the next morning, it's dark outside, but I manage to rise out of bed so I can make it to my morning yoga session. While I begin to fight myself and make excuses not to go, I tell myself it will help me relax. I shower, dress, and leave the apartment. Walking slowly down the sidewalk, I have a difficult time moving my body. I arrive just in time for class to begin and spread my yoga mat out in the back of the studio.

As Leanna leads us through our session for the day, I

have an even more difficult time concentrating on my body than I did when I was nervous for my first date with Jacob. Today, my body isn't shaking from anxiety; it's trembling because I'm struggling to hold together the pieces of my broken heart. I'm far from relaxed, and as I try to force my muscles to ease, they become even tenser.

When Leanna leads us down into child's pose, I stay there, unmoving, as the rest of the class continues into new poses. My mind is still racing, analyzing everything I know about Jacob. He seemed like a nice enough guy, but the way my body is responding to the thought of him, the more tense I become. I'm struck with fear. Fear of Jacob? Fear that he lied to me? That he's writing a story on me? I don't even know anymore.

As I pack up my belongings, I catch a glimpse of Jasmine and Abby, the girls I normally talk with at the beginning of the class. They steal a few glances at me. I try to ignore it, but I have to pass them to get out the door.

"Siobhan," Jasmine stops me. "Are you okay?"

"Do you want to go get a coffee or something?" Abby asks.

I guess they were watching me because they felt bad. I'm not entirely sure how awful I look, but I assume I look pretty heart broken.

I'm grateful for their offer, and it's nice to know they care, but I kindly refuse. "Sorry, but maybe some other time. I'm just not up to it today. Thanks."

Jasmine shoots a nervous glance at Abby. "Okay, Siobhan. Just let us know if you ever need some girl talk."

"Sure," I reply, but I don't think I'll ever be able to talk to these girls. I mean, I can hardly open up to Juliet about my problems. How can I talk with these girls I've only known for a few months? They're nice and all, and we've grabbed coffee after yoga classes before, but I just don't want to let them in on this.

After my yoga session, I return home and crawl back into bed. I'm grateful that Juliet has already left for work because I catch a glimpse of myself in the mirror, and I do *not* look good. My hair is a mess, and my face is bright red. I see what Jasmine and Abby were talking about now. I quickly look away, not wanting to face myself.

I really liked this guy—hell, I thought I might love him —and he turned out to be worse than any other guy I dated. I certainly got more than I bargained for with this man, and I don't want to speak to him again.

I mull these thoughts over in my mind, and I just can't take it anymore. I should not be wasting my time crying over some bastard who doesn't give a shit about who I really am.

I get out of bed and try my hardest to put Jacob out of my mind as I dive into my work. My efforts start to take effect, and I nearly forget about Jacob as I tend to my tasks. When I take a break from my clients to update my social media accounts and my blog, I discover several very upsetting things.

First, my mother's latest status announces how proud she is of her youngest daughter for getting engaged. This is the first thing that sets me off. My mother never praised me, and realizing this, my self-esteem plummets to the ground. It probably has to do with the fact that I've never accomplished anything.

Sure, you might say that becoming a celebrity before you're finished with your first decade of life is a huge accomplishment, but my parents didn't even want me to act. Of course, my mom and dad supported me in my dreams, taking me to auditions, classes, and rehearsals, but they didn't boast about my talent, let alone *praise* me. All of my praise came from my costars and fans.

Don't get me wrong. My parents weren't horrible people. They never took any of the money I made. They kept it in a trust fund for me until I turned eighteen, but it always seemed like I was struggling for their approval.

Even when I graduated with my degree, they didn't come out to support me because my sister was graduating from high school at the same time. It sucked they had to choose between us, but it still bites.

My body flames, and I ball my hands into fits without consciously trying to. I curse my sister for finding a great guy while I'm stuck here lonely and heart broken. I hide my mother's post. It's not even a minute later when a new issue strikes.

The next thing that gets at me is the red notification flag. When I click on it, it tells me that Jacob Bishop has accepted my friend request. Not only that, but he has also sent me a relationship request.

That bastard! I quickly go to his profile and unfriend him, blocking him in the process.

I push thoughts of him aside, and I become more productive as the day wears on.

I make the mistake of taking a break from my work, and it leaves me time to think again. With thoughts flying through my mind, I create a new blog post.

What Do You Do About Love?

By Siobhan Spencer

You know when you fall for a guy and he ends up being a complete bastard? Yes, you know what I'm talking about. You've been there, too.

Well, what do you do when you can't get him out of your mind? What do you do about love?

P.S. Is ten hours enough time to fall in love with someone?

I know this simple post is all I need, and soon enough, my followers are going to begin raiding my comment section with answers. All I can hope for is that I stumble across a few spectacular pieces of advice.

I push my glasses up my face, and I'm ready to get back to work.

I hear a buzz come from my dresser, and then my phone chimes. I rise, not sure what to expect from it because few people ever text me. When I check it, it's a text from Mackenzie. I open the message, and I see that she hasn't just sent a text, but there's a photo attached.

This is the dress Mom and I picked out yesterday. Can you believe I'm getting married!?
-M

No, no I cannot. I bite my lower lip and narrow my eyes at the screen. My sister, who is four years younger than me, is getting married before I am. I kind of hate her. Not only is she getting married, but she looks spectacular in her wedding dress, and she actually has the boobs to hold up the goddamn strapless beauty.

I throw my phone onto the bed, but it bounces and smashes against the wall. The hard protective case pops off of it. All the pieces fall to the mattress. I leave it there and get back to work.

At the moment, I'm not even considering my anger issues. It's not *me* with the problem. It's Mackenzie and her goddamn fairytale life. I tell myself this, but I know deep down that I don't believe it. What is my problem? I should be happy for Mackenzie, shouldn't I? The whole situation just seems so unfair, though.

I work for several more hours, hoping that nothing else will cause an outburst. I just don't want to deal with any of this right now. Why can't I rewind to two weeks ago and simply enjoy a night out at a club with Juliet instead of crawling beneath my sheets and crying over a man who faked his interest in me?

I'm shocked when the doorbell rings around three o'clock. I'm confused, not knowing exactly what to expect, but with my bad mood, I suspect that I won't like it. When I open the door, a boy—probably about nineteen—holding a bouquet of red roses stands in the hallway. I know immediately who sent them.

"Siobhan Spencer," the delivery boy says. He butchers my first name. I don't even bother correcting him.

It's a different guy from last time, but he's wearing the same attire as the man who delivered the yellow roses. He's thin with a boyish look to his face, and he gives a friendly smile.

"I don't want them," I snap, taking my anger out on this young man who clearly doesn't deserve it.

He takes a step back. "I'm just the delivery guy."

"Fine," I grit my teeth, and I snatch the roses from him. Back inside the apartment, I take the few steps to the kitchen and stop at the breakfast bar. Frantically, I search around for a crushing device, and my eyes fall upon the meat tenderizer in Juliet's collection of kitchen utensils. I grip it tightly in my hand, lay the bouquet of roses on the counter, and I smash away, taking my frustration out on yet another living thing that isn't at fault.

When I'm done, I take a step back and admire my handiwork. The roses bleed across the counter top.

Take that! I shout in my mind, and I think about how this scene so accurately represents the way my heart feels at this moment. I feel powerful after obliterating the gift. I give the roses a few more whacks before returning the meat tenderizer to its proper position on the counter.

I sweep the crushed roses into the garbage can and finally realize that there's a note attached to one of the stems. Curious, I read it.

Thanks for last weekend. Looking forward to tomorrow.
-Jacob

Thinking fast, I dig through one of the drawers in the kitchen where we keep our matches. I strike one of them against the box, and it ignites. I hold Jacob's note over the flame until it lights, and then I set it on the counter, watching the edges wither away to ash. I once again notice how the situation so closely bears a resemblance to my broken heart.

When there's no paper left to burn, I toss as much of the mess into the trash as I can, and then I wet a wash cloth and wipe down the crime scene, leaving no trace of evidence on the counter top.

I'm satisfied, feeling as if I've sufficiently earned my revenge.

CHAPTER FOURTEEN

WHEN JULIET ARRIVES BACK at the apartment, she sees that my bedroom door is open and takes this opportunity to finally speak to me. Thank God I didn't leave the crushed roses on the counter. Then she'd really have something to inquire about, and I don't want to talk about any of it.

"You totally got laid," she sings. "Jacob had that post-sex glow to him today. It was so obvious. I told you that you two would hit it off."

I glare at her.

"What's wrong? Wasn't it good?"

"Let's just say there won't be a third date," I state bluntly. I'm again taking my anger out on someone who doesn't deserve it.

Or maybe she does... She's the one who set us up.

She takes a step back and holds her hands up.

"Okay," she says, elongating the vowels. "Clearly

someone has something up her ass, although I don't understand why. Jacob seemed happy enough."

"Yeah, well, he shouldn't," I hiss, hoping my tone will make her leave me alone. I really don't want to talk about Jacob right now. In fact, I don't want to talk about him ever. He already has enough information from me for his story.

"Look, Siobhan, whatever your problem is, you might want to talk to him. He really likes you, and he's expecting a third date."

Great. So she's talked to him, and he's confided in her. What is he playing at? And sending me those goddamn flowers? What right does he have?

"I really think you should talk to him." She makes it sound like a suggestion, but I know she's trying to make it into a command.

"I really think you should mind your own goddamn business. Don't bother setting me up with anyone *ever* again." I rise from my computer and grasp the corner of my door.

Juliet stands in the doorway, but she backs away. Once she's free of the door's swing, I slam it. I can hear her muttering to herself behind it. "What's *her* problem?"

As I'm tending to my blog comments and terribly unsatisfied with the answers I'm receiving for my latest post, I hear Juliet through my wall talking to someone. I only overhear her voice, and I know she's on the phone. I ignore it at first until I catch my name, and then I press my ear against the wall to eavesdrop on her.

"I don't *know*. Siobhan won't tell me anything. She just

slammed the door in my face." She pauses for a moment, listening to the person on the other end. "No, she said she didn't want a third date with you. Jacob, what happened between you guys?" Pause. "I know, you two seemed so happy the other day, and I thought you two really hit it off." Pause. "Well, it's a mystery to me, too. Maybe you should call her." Pause. "Okay, bye."

Juliet stops speaking, and I know she's hung up. A few moments later, my phone comes to life and begins buzzing. I know who's calling without looking, but I pick it up off my bed where it's still lying and check it anyway. The caller ID says Jacob Bishop, and I hit the end button before he has a chance to leave a voicemail.

I hear Juliet's phone ring in the other room, and I press my ear against the wall again.

"Hey," she greets, pausing to let Jacob speak. "Yeah, I'll go talk to her."

Moments later, there's a knock at my door.

"Go away!" I shout.

"Come on, Siobhan," she says through the door. "Would you just tell me what's up? I think Jacob has a right to know why you've recently broke up with him. I know you two slept together. Was it that?"

"God, no!" I practically screech. "The sex was great, it's just... Juliet, I can't trust him."

"Oh, I see," she says accusingly. "So it's nothing *he* did. It's your goddamn trust issues."

My trust issues? What is she talking about? I do not have trust issues. I have a problem with people like Jacob, people who lie and cheat for no good reason but for an article.

"I suggest you go talk to him about whatever problem you're having," Juliet insists. "He's just as confused as I am."

Confused? Is he possibly confused that I figured out his plan? I knew there was no reason for a guy like that to be with a girl like me. I'd raised my hopes too high. It was simply too good to be true, and for a moment, I lost myself in it. I will *never* do that again.

I don't even know why Juliet cares so much.

"Just *talk* to him," she begs.

"Fine." I grit my teeth. I fling my door open and stare at Juliet. "I'll go *talk* to him."

Oh, I'll go talk to him, but not the way Juliet is expecting. I'm going to confront him and tell him *exactly* how I feel. I push past Juliet, grab my purse, and leave the apartment, slamming the door behind me. I don't care to pay attention to how I look. I'm sure my hair is a mess, and I'm still wearing my glasses.

I'm suddenly very brave, and perhaps that has something to do with the adrenaline racing through my system. The sensation travels with me all the way to his apartment. My fists clench along the way, and my lips press into a hard line. Who does this guy think he is? What's wrong with people like this? Why would he go so far for a girl like me? I'm nothing special. God, I wish people like this would just leave me alone.

As these thoughts pound on the walls of my skull, I

form a tension headache. Somehow, I maintain my courage as I catch the door to his building as another resident is leaving.

It's not difficult to find apartment 202. With all my rage, I pound on his door. When the door opens, a small boy stands in front of me.

I'm left in complete shock, and I know all the color has drained from my face. I may have believed that I knocked on the wrong apartment door if the young toddler staring up at me wasn't the spitting image of Jacob.

CHAPTER FIFTEEN

A *KID*! Jacob has a mother-fucking *kid*! I may have left out a small detail about my past, but this is inexcusable. The kid looks *just* like him.

My face falls, and I'm too overwhelmed by this newfound knowledge that I turn and flee.

I hear Jacob behind me. "Who is it, kiddo?" he asks his son, and I hear the door open wider.

I'm booking my way out of there, but when he catches a glimpse of my auburn hair disappearing around the corner, he comes chasing after me.

I was furious at him before, but now I'm even more angry and upset that he's following me. A *child*! What else is he hiding? I really don't want to find out.

"Siobhan!" he shouts.

I quicken my pace. I can already feel the tears welling up inside of me, and the knot in my chest tightens.

He catches me on the staircase, gripping my wrist. I

whirl around to face him. He simply stares at me for a moment, and his eyes scan my face with an expression I can't read.

"What—what's wrong?" he asks.

Like you don't know, I want to scream. I feel the tears coming, and I know there's a crease forming between my eyebrows. What must I look like to him? I imagine that my irises are bright red and that flame is shooting out my ears. That's how I feel, at least.

I want to yell at him, to scream at the top of my lungs and let him know exactly how unfair he was to me, but I can't muster up the energy.

"Why?" I whisper in a soft, almost non-existent voice. I don't feel as if the tone of my voice accurately exhibits my emotions. Instead of anger, my voice holds a tone of sadness and betrayal behind it. Perhaps that's how I really feel. I'm not sure.

His eyes scan my face. "Siobhan, I don't know what I did wrong. Why don't you come back to my apartment and we'll talk it out?"

He embraces me, and I feel warm against his body, yet the hug seems to crush my heart even further. I don't want him to hug me, but I let him anyway. I don't push against him like my body is begging me to do. I don't say anything as he leads me to his apartment and sets me on his love seat.

His apartment is small. The kitchen is just big enough for two people to stand in, and his living room is about half the size of mine. The room houses a loveseat, a recliner, a small coffee table, and a television. On the coffee table sits a laptop and a few magazines. Other than that, the place is tidy. It doesn't look like a guy lives here. It looks more like a family does.

The living room and the kitchen are open to each other, similar to my apartment only more condensed. Beyond this space, there are three doors.

Jacob's son is sitting in the recliner looking up at us. I'm guessing he's about four years old.

"Ben," Jacob says gently, "to your room please."

"But—" the child begins to argue.

"No *buts*. We need a moment alone." Jacob points to one of the doors. I'm stunned by his authoritative tone. It's so... father-like.

Ben's shoulders fall. "Fine," he says as he crawls down from the recliner and enters one of the doors. I'm guessing that the other two are Jacob's bedroom and the bathroom.

Once the child is gone, Jacob kneels beside me, putting his face at my level. He tries looking into my eyes, but I avoid his gaze.

He speaks softly. "Siobhan, please tell me what's wrong. I can tell it's hard for you to open up to people, but I want to help. Whatever it is, I can take it."

I jerk my face up at him, tearing my gaze from the spot on the floor I was staring at. "Oh, please. Like you don't know," I hiss.

He stays calm and collected, and I hate him for that. Why can't I ever stay calm and collected? He shakes his head slowly. "Honestly, Siobhan, I have no idea what's going on."

How can he not know what's going on? I think. There are so many things I'm mad about right now. And... a kid? Why does he act like that's no big deal? Maybe I'm going crazy. Maybe he told me about Ben and I wasn't listening. Am I that insane that I blocked it out?

"Let's start with this one," I snarl. "How about the article you wrote on how to please a woman? How many women *exactly* have you slept with?"

I don't know why I focus on this detail first. It really shouldn't even matter to me. Perhaps I do it because it's the easiest one to handle at the moment, and I'm upset about it because I don't want to be taken advantage of by a player. It kills me to think last night meant nothing to him.

"Is that what this is about?" His voice is still even and calm. "You think I sleep around?"

He's waiting for an answer.

"I'm not sure what to think right now." My voice goes quiet again.

"Siobhan, I'm not afraid to be honest with you. I don't normally sleep with women on the second date. I may have twenty-seven years under my belt, but I don't have many girls to count."

"How many?" I whisper, and I'm afraid of the answer. He seemed so much more experienced than me, and I'm frightened of this. I focus in on it mostly because I don't want to face the bigger issue—the story that he's writing about me.

"Including you? Four."

I'm stunned. Only one more than me. Perhaps he's lying to me again. He notices my surprise, and I can tell he knows I don't quite believe in his low number.

"I don't sleep with a girl unless I really like her," he explains.

I find myself looking into this deeply, perhaps too deeply. Does that mean he *does* really like me? How long does it take to really like someone? How long did it take for him to sleep with these other women? Or is he just saying this to get more out of me?

I've never had luck when it comes to romance. I've never been in a serious relationship. It's ridiculous to admit it to myself, but I've never felt for someone the way I feel about Jacob, or at least the way I felt about him earlier this week. God, I don't even know the guy. How can I have fallen for him? It doesn't make any sense.

I ponder if Jacob has ever been serious with someone, but I already know the answer to that judging by the kid in the next room, the one who looks just like him.

"Have you ever been in a serious relationship?" I ask, stalling the reason I really came here.

"It depends on what you mean by serious. I have been in long-term relationships, but I've never been serious enough for marriage."

Apparently, one of them had been serious enough to have a kid with. I wonder if she's still a part of his life. God, I don't want to think about that.

"What about the article about childhood stars? The

one that shows the pictures of actors when they're children and what they look like now?" I ask.

His eyebrows come together, forming a crease above his nose. "It was just an assignment."

"Is that what I am to you?" I demand, shooting to my feet. "An *assignment*?"

He rises with me. "No, absolutely not."

I don't believe him. His voice remains steady. God, how does he stay so calm?

"You can't honestly stand here and tell me you don't know who I am!" I clench my fists.

"I have no idea what you're talking about." He still seems calm, and I don't believe a word he's saying.

"Drop the act. I also saw your article about Elizabeth River."

"I don't know what you're getting at, but those articles were just assignments. My clients tell me what to write, and I make shit up. Same with the other article about pleasing women."

"Make shit up," I snap. "Is that what you're planning to do with me? To *make shit up*!?"

His voice grows louder. "What the *hell* are you talking about?"

"You're telling me that you don't know who I am?"

His eyes study me for a moment, moving across my face. He shakes his head and with a quiet voice says, "No."

I don't believe him. I just can't. If he hadn't heard of me before, surely he would have searched my name online before meeting me. He would have ran across hundreds of articles about my childhood, not to mention my blog that mentions my acting career.

I grab the laptop off the coffee table, plopping myself back down in my spot.

He seems confused, but he doesn't protest. He lets me continue. I open the laptop and search my name.

A long list of search results appears. My Wikipedia biography is at the top followed by a link to my blog, various interviews, and pages dedicated to the movies I've been in. I click on the tab at the top titled "Images," and I come face to face with myself.

The images span the entire page. Most of them are of me as a young girl between the ages of four and seven. Some of them are snapshots of the characters I played, and others are of me on the red carpet. There are a few pictures of an older me that have found their way to Google via my blog or public profiles. I don't like looking at these pictures, and I normally avoid them at all costs.

"Have fun," I growl, shoving the laptop his way.

I regret coming here at all, and I no longer want to tell him how I feel. I want to get out of here as soon as possible and forget that Jacob and I were ever together. An assignment? Am I one of his *assignments*? What is he playing at, pretending that he doesn't know? And what's with the kid in the next room that apparently isn't a big deal, either? This man makes no sense.

I rise from the couch as he stares into my past via the computer screen. I head for the door. Before I can close the short distance between the love seat and the front door, however, it swings open. It takes a few moments for me to process what's in the doorway.

In walks a gorgeous tall blonde with beauty comparable to Juliet's, although they don't look the same. This woman is dressed in business attire with a slimming suit coat and matching skirt. Her nylon tights and shiny black high heels finish off her ensemble, and her flowing blonde hair complements it all. She even has highlights and a mother-fucking tan. Jacob may not have to compete with anyone from my past, but I don't have anything on this girl. She's simply stunning.

She's carrying in bags of groceries and seems shocked to see me. The woman stares past me to Jacob.

I stop dead in my tracks. It takes a few seconds for me to realize I'm holding my breath.

"Where's Ben?" she demands, and I understand who she is immediately. This is Ben's mother.

"He's in his room," Jacob answers.

"And who's *she*?" the woman snarls, sticking her chin in my direction.

I quickly analyze the way she's carrying in the groceries and how she looks at me accusingly, and I realize that this woman lives here. It doesn't take long for me to process that there are only two bedrooms in this apartment and that Ben occupies one of them.

The knot in my chest tightens to a point where I'm convinced it's attempting to strangle me. I hate Jacob right now. How could he lie to me like this? How could he cheat on a woman for the sake of a story? How can he just sit there and pretend that none of this is a big deal?

He's certainly the award-winning actor—not me.

I finally regain control of my body and push past the woman. I want to put as much distance in between us as possible. I race down the hall.

"God damn it, Jen," I hear Jacob snap at the woman, and seconds later, his footsteps are coming after me.

Tears stream down my face as I pound down the stairs as fast as I can.

"Siobhan!" Jacob shouts after me, and I know he's getting close.

I whirl around to face him, and he stops dead in his tracks.

"Please, let me explain," he begs.

I shake my head. "I don't want to hear it. Damn it, Jacob, I *trusted* you. I made love to you. Don't you *ever* come near me again."

There's an older woman—maybe in her sixties— walking up the stairs as I say this, and she stares at us in shock. I despise the way she's glaring at me as if I've done something wrong.

"Fuck off," I growl at her.

With that, I turn and storm away. Jacob doesn't chase after me this time.

CHAPTER SIXTEEN

I'M STILL FLAMING when I arrive home. Juliet is in the living room. She sees my tears and bounces up from her spot on the couch with a frown on her face.

"My God, Siobhan. What happened?"

"I don't want to talk about it." I know I'm being a bitch to her again. I enter my room and slam the door before I fall to my bed.

Juliet speaks to me through the closed door. "Did you two at least talk?"

"Yeah, Juliet, we talked. No, Juliet, it didn't help. If anything, it made things worse. God, just stay out of it and mind your own fucking business. You're the one who got me into this mess!"

I hear her footsteps retreat. She doesn't bother me the rest of the night.

I bury my face into my pillow. I thought I was in love with Jacob, and then I find out that he's not only possibly writing a story about me but that he has a kid and that he *lives* with his kid's mother. That's not something I can forgive. Is that why he had to leave early for each date? Is it because he didn't want his girlfriend to find out? Their relationship must be bad if he cheated on her with *me*.

I feel dirty thinking about this, realizing I'm *that* girl. I've never been *that* girl, and I really don't want to be. Why would he invite me into his apartment if he knew his girlfriend would be home soon? Maybe she came home early and that's why he shouted at her when I left. I find myself wondering what's going on between them, and I imagine they're fighting.

"Who is she?" Jen says in my head.

"She's no one," Jacob replies in his calm, collected manner.

"Oh, really? She's the slut you've been seeing, isn't she? And you let her in here with Ben in the next room. How could you, Jake?"

I don't like the way my fantasy is going, so I quickly repress this thought and try not to worry about what happened after I left.

Why did I have to accept Juliet's invitation to go meet this guy? Sure, I had the time of my life when I was with him, but I hate him for lying to me.

As I lie awake in my bed, I try my hardest to let go of him. That bastard has no right tearing apart my heart like this. Who does he think he is?

I don't want him to affect me like this, and I struggle to regain control over my body, to sooth the knot in my chest and relieve my heart ache, but the more I try, the worse it gets. I can't let go of this man. He was so good to me for a moment, and I know I will never forget that.

I cry long enough that the tears stop coming. I now have a hard film across my face where they've dried up. I wipe it away with my hands the best I can.

When I regain a bit of strength, I realize how empty my stomach is, and although I have no appetite, I know I have to eat something. I can't remember the last time I ate.

I exit my bedroom and enter the darkness of the apartment. Juliet has gone to bed, and I can only navigate my way around via the light seeping in through the living room window.

I open the fridge and find nothing. I really need to go grocery shopping. That thought takes me back to earlier today when Jen walked through the door with her groceries, and it makes my skin burn with rage as I replay the memory.

A box in the back of the fridge catches my eye. I pull it out and open it. It's the piece of pizza from our second date, all cold and dried up. I know it would taste fine if I put it in the microwave, but I really don't want to it eat, so I throw it out.

I grab the milk carton from the top shelf and dig in the cupboards for a box of cereal. I pull my dish from the drying rack next to the sink and prepare myself a bowl, finishing off the milk. I look down at my first scoop, staring at the shooting star marshmallow in the dim light. I could really use a wish, and although it's childish, I wish upon this shooting star, praying that this situation will somehow work its way out.

I finish my cereal and return to my bedroom, removing my glasses and crawling back into bed where it seems I've been spending most of my time lately.

When I wake up, I feel a little better. I put myself into my work to get my mind off of Jacob. I almost succeed until the doorbell rings.

Not again, I think to myself, and I nervously make my way to the door. When I open it, I'm not surprised at what I see. There's a bouquet of flowers—red roses again—waiting for me, but when the delivery guy hands me the bouquet, he also puts a large box of chocolates in my hand.

Curiosity gets the better of me, and I check the note that Jacob's left me. It's a simple message.

I'm sorry.
-Jacob

I haven't forgiven him, but I don't take the meat tenderizer to these flowers this time. Instead, I simply toss them in the garbage. I keep the chocolates and place them next to me on my computer desk. I eat them, mostly because they were free, and I find comfort in the assortment of flavors. Each delicious piece melts in my mouth, but I don't let them remind me of Jacob.

I continue throughout my week by diving into web design, and I find that it easily takes my mind off things. That is, when Jacob isn't sending me flowers.

On Wednesday, I'm able to relax better in my yoga session and even chat with my normal group of friends before class, but when I get home and the doorbell rings, my body tenses. His note this time:

Please Call.
-Jacob

I delete his number from my phone, which now has a slight crack in the screen from when I threw it across the room. I won't make the mistake of actually calling him. Instead, I want to forget all about him.

When I finally have enough courage to face Juliet, she asks me how I'm doing.

"I'm fine," I tell her.

"Are you finally ready to tell me what you've been upset about?" Her voice is calm, collected, and full of sincere concern for me. It annoys me.

"No," I snap at her, and she drops the subject. I know I'm being a bitch again, but I just don't want to deal with this shit.

A while later, I catch Juliet texting. I know she's talking to Jacob about me. A knife cuts into my back, and I feel betrayed by her for talking to the bastard.

I wished she'd never set us up in the first place.

CHAPTER SEVENTEEN

WHEN THURSDAY ARRIVES, my heart is still aching for him. The week is seeming to go by at snail pace when I think about my aching heart, but when I look at anything else, it feels like it's passing at lightning speed. It's disorienting.

I get out of bed and sit at my computer desk. As my computer takes its sweet time turning on, I swivel in my chair.

It's now that I notice the bits of Jacob still spread across my room. His sticky notes from Sunday are still stuck to my desk where I left them. The first bouquet of flowers that he sent are still in the trash next to my desk, wilted and dead. The note attached to one of the stems stares up at me from the pile of glass shards. Underneath the flowers and the note sits his used condom. The two boxes of chocolate he sent, both empty, also lie on my computer desk as a reminder.

I abruptly crumple up his sticky notes and throw them in the trash followed by the chocolate boxes. Then I gather up the trash bag at the corners and tie the plastic edges together.

I take the bag to the kitchen and toss it in the garbage. There. Now there's nothing left to remind me of him.

With this action and feeling of accomplishment, I realize I've been working far too much lately. I give myself permission to simply take the day off to relax, but I don't stay in the apartment. Instead, I get dressed, slipping on a pair of comfortable jeans and a white tee. I throw my hair up in a high ponytail, avoiding the mirror as I do so, grab my purse, and exit the apartment.

I flag down a taxi and ride to Central Park. I need to relax, and I think a bit of nature might do the trick. Once I arrive at the edge of the park, I climb out of the taxi and hand the cab driver some cash. Then I stroll into the trees.

The sun is bright today, and the air temperature is in perfect sync with my body, not too hot and not too cold. The light breeze adds the finishing touches to the perfect weather. The smell of the city soothes me.

I take a lengthy walk along the paths, trying to calm my body by taking in the scenery while focusing on the trees. For the first time all week, I start to feel relaxed. The knot in my chest begins to loosen, and my tension headache starts to let up.

After several hours of walking nearly every path in the park, I find a bench and rest upon it, closing my eyes and listening to the sounds around me. It really is quite soothing. The knot in my chest loosens even further, and I feel a bit better about myself.

As I listen to the sounds around me, I hear hooves on the pavement. I look up to find a beautiful white carriage headed my way. My heart drops as I admire the couple in the cab and the way the guy has his arm around her. The girl is smiling up at him. It reminds me of the way Jacob and I enjoyed a moment like this not even a week ago.

I'm momentarily pulled from my serene state as I stare at the couple, but once they pass and are out of sight, I close my eyes again and allow my body to relax.

I know I've been here for a while—all day it seems— and when I feel I've had sufficient time to unwind, I reach into my purse and pull out my cellphone to check the time.

My hand grazes across a piece of paper I don't remember putting in my bag. When I pull it out to see what it is, my heart flips inside my chest. I'm not sure if the sensation is a feeling of happiness that takes me back to the moment these photos were taken, if it's a feeling of loss for not being able to keep this happy moment within my grasp, or if it's a feeling of disappointment and hurt that I still have these photos in my possession.

It's the photo strip from the booth that Jacob and I went to on Saturday. The corner is crumpled from being in my purse, but I smooth it out. I study the photos, and in them, I look so happy. I want that sort of happiness back, but I'm not sure if I'll ever find it again.

Jacob is smiling up at me, too. When I get to the bottom snapshot, the one where I caught him off guard with a kiss, I actually let out a giggle, amused by his expression. I quickly repress my giggle and continue studying the photograph.

Unwilling to see Jacob's face, I cover each of his four expressions with my right hand, and I focus only on my own face. I look spectacular, and it's not because I worked extra hard to make my hair look nice or to match the perfect shade of blush to my otherwise colorless cheeks. I look stunning because of the expression on my face, which is one of joy and happiness. I can tell I'm enjoying myself in these photos.

I flip the photo strip over in my hand, and on the back is the last note I have left from Jacob.

I exit the park, still thinking about Jacob and clutching the photograph. I flag down another taxi.

When I climb in, the cab driver asks, "Where to, ma'am?"

I am unable to answer. I sit in silence for a moment, not sure where I'm headed.

"Ma'am?" he asks again.

I'm shocked by what comes out of my mouth next. "I want to go back to the Ferris wheel," I say, more to myself than to the driver.

"I'm sorry, but you're going to have to be more specific."

I wish I could be, but when Jacob took me there, I never watched where we were going, and it was my first time there. I don't know where it is.

"I don't know the address," I tell him.

"Well, you're going to have to give me something." He seems annoyed, but he keeps his friendly smile.

I do my best to describe the place to him, and after a few descriptors, he knows where he's headed. We ride in silence, and I'm surprised to see it's already getting dark out. I was walking through the park for quite some time, and I estimate I was sitting on my bench for several hours.

When the taxi stops, I recognize the place, and I know this is exactly where the cab dropped us off last time. I hand the driver my money and thank him, exiting the vehicle.

It's getting dark enough that the Ferris wheel's lights are now on. I marvel at the beauty of it. This scene is simply stunning. I take out my phone and snap a picture, remembering a few of the pointers Jacob showed me the other day in Central Park. I take a few moments to study the photo, and I'm satisfied.

I make my way to the Ferris wheel, and when it's my turn in line, I hand the guy enough cash for one ride. I climb into the seat by myself, and in no time, I'm rising above the city.

More and more lights brighten the city, and they intensify as the sun goes down. By now, the sun is touching the horizon and shining over the water in a spectacular manner that leaves me awestruck. It's simply stunning from up here, and the corners of my mouth actually turn up into a smile, which I allow to transform into a grin.

The wheel makes another revolution, and as I near the top, I spread my arms out as if I'm flying. I feel free up here, and I'm in love with the metropolis. My repressed smile erupts into a full grin as I fly above the city.

It doesn't make sense that I'm here, and I know that, but I find some comfort in it anyway. When the man at the bottom releases me from my seat, I exit the ride unsure of what to do next. I stroll between the vendors along the water, hoping for some inspiration to strike.

The first concession that catches my eye is the cotton candy booth I went to on Saturday. I approach the counter and pay for my order. I pull off a piece of cotton candy and taste it. It melts in my mouth, reminding me of Jacob's kisses. I let it sit there until it fully dissolves.

I easily find an empty space on the lawn, and I sit down, depositing my cotton candy into my mouth slowly while I admire the changing scenery around me. The sun has set now, but it's still illuminating the atmosphere. I focus on the city lights as the sky dims, and I'm completely lost in the artwork of the city.

It's exquisite from this point of view, and all the city lights in all the skyscrapers combine together effortlessly to create a beautiful work of art.

Even after I'm done with my cotton candy and the air begins to cool, I still marvel at the city. I really needed this day to relax, and with the aid of the city lights, the tension within my body eases. I'm now feeling more confident, freeing most of my anxiety from my mind.

Feeling like I've had enough time here, I get up, throw out my cotton candy stick, and wave down a taxi.

Before I slide into my seat, I turn around one last time,

take in the beauty, and snap a photo of the brilliant Ferris wheel against the dark background.

I stare down at the photo as the taxi driver pulls away. My heart twists in my chest. In that moment, it becomes abundantly clear that it doesn't matter how much I try to distance myself by throwing away his things or taking time alone to feel better.

No amount of time in the world could make me forget about Jacob Bishop.

CHAPTER EIGHTEEN

I FEEL BETTER on Friday morning. As lunch approaches and I check the time on my laptop, I also catch a glimpse of the date. Tonight is the opening reception for the art exhibit that one of Juliet's paintings will be in. I'm grateful for this, because I really need a night out.

I'm already dressed in a red evening gown and ready to go before Juliet gets home. My dress is gorgeous, with beaded embellishments around my cleavage. The straps crisscross the back, leaving most of my spine exposed. The dress is long enough to trail along the floor, but with my black heels on, it just grazes the ground. There's a slit up the side that exposes my leg, and I've completed this look by curling my hair and piling it to the side, adding bright red lipstick to finish off my ensemble. I'm pleased with my appearance for once and force a bit of a smile in the mirror.

Juliet enters the door and gawks at me. "You look *hot!*" she compliments.

"Thanks!" I say as Juliet makes her way to her room to get ready.

When she finally emerges from her bedroom, she looks even sexier than I do. Her yellow dress is the perfect shade to complement her blonde hair and tan complexion. It's a single-strapped dress, and all the fabric comes to bunch onto the opposite side of the strap with a jeweled embell-ishment to hold it in place. The dress falls to her feet, and her hair is piled atop her head in a beautiful updo.

"Juliet, *you* look hot."

She grins and spins around, letting me see her from every angle. I know she's excited for the exhibit. I smile back at her, happy for her accomplishment. She really deserves this with all the hard work she puts into her paint-ings and showing off other artists' works. Tonight, though, it's her turn to shine a bit, even if it is just one painting.

"Shall we?" she asks, and we exit together and make our way to Pierceton's Galleries, the location of her displayed painting. I don't bring anything along with me except some cash in case I need it.

When we get to the gallery, there are already people shuffling into the building. We make our way inside, and the art seems to go on for miles. It's a labyrinth in here, and I'm amazed that Juliet was able to get her artwork put into a show this huge.

I'm hoping Juliet understands what an accomplish-ment this is. She hasn't said much about the exhibit at all, but perhaps I just haven't been listening. I've been acting like a selfish bitch lately, and I'm a bit annoyed at myself for it. Tonight, however, I'm not going to let anything bother me.

After a moment, Juliet sees someone she knows, and I let her run off and make conversation as I explore the maze of artwork surrounding me. Immersing myself into it, I take my time to admire each painting by different artists.

One painting in particular catches my eye, and I let myself get lost in it for several minutes. It's a painting of a glorious landscape that depicts the setting sun over a beautiful lake. It's not the landscape that captivates me, though. It's the magnificent brush stroke that makes the sun's reflection off the water come to life and appear as if in motion. Something about the painting seems familiar, and when I check the caption, I know why.

This is Juliet's work of art, and although I've seen her talent before, I can't pull my eyes away from it. I'm forced to, however, when a man with a tray of Champaign glasses walks up to me.

"Champaign?" he asks.

I graciously accept, taking a glass from his tray. I sip on it, and it tastes sweet.

I'm still admiring the painting when another man walks up to me. He's older and slim with a grey mustache. He doesn't say anything for a few moments as he admires the painting along with me.

He finally breaks the silence. "Beautiful, isn't it?"

I look at him, then back at the painting. "Yeah, it really is."

"This artist has real talent," he compliments as he turns away to view other paintings, and I'm excited by his words.

I want to tell Juliet what he's said, so I turn from the painting to go find her. This is such a huge accomplishment, and I want her to know exactly how amazing this is for her.

I'm not sure precisely where I am. I'm still lost between the walls in the maze. I shuffle between stand-alone walls and pieces of artwork in the center of the aisles, trying to remember how exactly I got so far back into the room.

I'm expecting to emerge into the entrance any time now, but when I round the corner, my excitement comes to a screeching halt. In front of me stands none other than Jacob Bishop. His elbow is propped up on his opposite hand, and he's studying the painting in front of him.

I turn, putting the wall between us, but he's already caught a glimpse of me. "Siobhan," he calls after me.

I freeze and press my body against the wall, trying to blend in. I'm hoping I'll turn invisible, but he catches up with me.

In an instant, all the effort I put into relaxing yesterday is rendered useless. My body tenses, and all my thoughts about Jacob come rushing back into my head.

"Look, can we talk about what happened?" he asks.

I want desperately to escape, but Jacob is so close to me now that I'm not sure if I can. I haven't yet mastered the ability to melt into walls, either. Nevertheless, I'm trying very hard to disappear. My heart races, and I'm just barely able squeak out my words.

"No, Jacob." I try to stay calm, but a bit of a snarl escapes my lips. "I don't want to talk."

He doesn't listen to me. "I understand you have difficulties trusting people, Siobhan. I get that now, and I don't blame you for not telling me about your past. It makes sense." His voice stays calm and quiet. "I just wish you could take a leap of faith on this one and trust me."

I'm fully annoyed at him. I hate that he's pushing the issue and that he's also blocking my escape route. He's so close to me now that I can smell him. Although I don't want to, I can't help but take a long inhale to enjoy his fragrance. Damn you, Jacob Bishop, for smelling so great.

After a moment, I realize what I'm doing, and I hold my breath.

"I don't want to talk," I say as I push past him, shoving him out of my way with my elbow. My face flames, and my fists clench in exasperation.

Why in God's name is he here? Did Juliet invite him just because I was coming? I'm mad. I'm upset at both of them, and without taking the time to find Juliet, I down the rest of my Champaign. Then I leave the gallery as quick as I can find my way out.

Once out in the night air, I stop and press my hands into my knees, bending at the waist. I try to pull in as much air as possible, but it's not making its way to my lungs. There's a pain in my chest, and I think I'm having a panic attack. I take another deep breath, and that seems to help.

After a few moments, I regain my strength, and I'm able to breathe again. There are a few people outside staring at me, but I ignore them.

I have no idea where I'm headed. All I know is that I want to distance myself from the gallery. My heels click against the sidewalk for what seems like quite a while. I'm drained of all my energy, so I slow, finally giving in and waving down a taxi. I give the cab driver my address, and we continue toward my apartment.

I stare out the window as we drive through the city streets, and I'm suddenly intrigued by the nightlife. Lights flash from every direction, and people crowd the sidewalks. The scene appears so enthralling right now, like I could easily get lost in it and forget about my troubles.

"Stop the cab!" I shout, and the driver pulls over. "Let me out here."

CHAPTER NINETEEN

PEOPLE SURROUND me from every angle, walking up and down the sidewalks, but what really catches my attention is the line of people forming at the entrance of a club. I suddenly want in.

It's been so long since Juliet and I went dancing. I remember weeks ago suggesting we go dancing after the art reception. It doesn't matter that she isn't here. I want to go.

Instead of waiting at the back of the line, I approach the bouncer at the front. I only want to ask him about how long it will take to get in, but before I can say anything, he unlatches the barrier and lets me pass. I hear the crowd groan behind me, but I don't care.

I'm shocked, until I realize maybe he recognizes me. I thank him, then continue down the hallway until I emerge into a massive room packed with people.

I almost forget about Jacob entirely once I'm inside. The music reverberates throughout my body, and before I know it, my hips are involuntarily swinging along to the beat.

I'm not exactly dressed for this type of nightlife, but I know I look hot. I make my way to the center of the dance floor and let my body sway along with the beat. As if the music is soaking up my sorrow, I slowly begin to let go. It doesn't take long until I dance away my bad mood.

I'm smiling now, and I'm not holding my body back. I feel like a goddess.

One guy watches me from a few people away, and I stare back at him. He's tall with a strong build and a smile to die for. His shirt is unbuttoned slightly so that I catch a glimpse of his chest. With our eyes locked, he makes his way toward me and shouts over the music.

"You alone tonight, baby?" he asks loud enough so I can hear him.

Without trying, our bodies press together due to the fact that there are so many people crowding the dance floor. We move against each other.

"Yep," I shout back.

"Good," he shouts over the music. "So no one will mind if I do this."

He wraps his arms around my waist and pulls me even closer to him. I don't mind. It takes my mind off of everything else.

I turn my body around so I'm facing away from the guy. My ass presses against him, and I grind against his body. I let my body move closer to the ground, bending at the knees, and then in one swift motion, I make my way back to a standing position, pressing my backside along his form the entire way.

This feels great. I don't recall a time that I've ever done this with a stranger. It's thrilling.

"Can I buy you a drink?" he asks, but I can't hear him over the music.

"What?" I shout back.

He raises his voice. "Can I buy you a drink?"

"I'd love one!"

He leads me off the dance floor and to the bar. He orders me a drink, yelling at the bartender over the music, but I can't hear what he's ordered. I'm a bit taken aback, and I think about how Jacob lets me order for myself. When the bartender places a shot glass in front of me, I down the sucker as soon as possible in hopes of erasing Jacob from my mind for the night. It burns on the way down.

The guy I've been dancing with—I never do get his name—swallows his own shot before we return to the dance floor together.

I dance with this guy until I am too tired to dance any longer. I figure I've been here for a couple of hours.

"I'm sorry," I lean up at him and shout into his ear so he can hear me. "I'm just too tired to keep dancing."

He doesn't seem disappointed by this. Instead, he leads me off the dance floor. Once we make our way to a less crowded area near the bar, he pulls me into him. Before I know it, he leans down and sticks his tongue down my throat.

What the hell? I try to push him away, but he only holds me tighter. My pulse quickens. When he finally pulls away, he speaks.

"Let me take you home." It sounds more like a demand than a question.

I take a step back. I'm not looking for a relationship of any sort, and I'm certainly not interested in a one-night stand. All I wanted to do was dance. This doesn't seem like the kind of guy who gets rejected often. I'm terrified of what will happen if I reject his offer.

I have to get out of here—*fast*. "I need to use the ladies' room first."

"I'll be right here waiting for you," he tells me with a seductive raise of his eyebrows.

I get out of there as soon as I can, slipping out the back door when he isn't watching. I'm in no place to get involved with someone, especially when I don't even know their name.

I quickly flag down a cab and head home. When I enter the apartment, Juliet is standing in the living room, her arms crossed, and her lips pressed into a hard line. She's already changed out of her dress, but her hair is still styled in her beautiful updo.

She explodes.

CHAPTER TWENTY

"WHERE THE *HELL* have you been? The reception ended hours ago, and when I went looking for you, you were just *gone.* Jacob said you left, and when I got back, you weren't here!"

"God." I roll my eyes. "I didn't know I needed *permission* to go out."

"I was worried about you, Siobhan. I had no idea where you were."

"What was Jacob even *doing* there? You should have told me he'd be there," I snap.

"He was there because he's my *friend,*" she bites back.

Tears well up in her eyes—a rarity for Juliet—and I suddenly realize why she wants Jacob and me together so badly. We're her friends, both of us, and she wants us to be happy. I can hear it in her tone that there is no other reason but that, and I know she really wanted this to work out.

"What's your issue with him, anyway?" she asks.

I start toward my bedroom door, not wanting to talk about it, but she steps in front of me, blocking my path.

"No. You're not hiding out in your room until you tell me what's going on." God, she can be so damn bossy sometimes.

"I said I don't want to talk about it," I snarl.

"You're never going to want to talk about it if you keep this up. Jacob told me about what happened at his apartment. Are you afraid of him because you think he knows about your childhood? First of all, Jacob *didn't* know until you told him, and second of all, he doesn't give a shit. He likes you, and you've sabotaged it."

"Juliet," I say in a soft, defeated voice. "He's written about celebrities before."

"New flash, Siobhan: you're not a celebrity anymore."

Her statement bites. I don't want her to be, but she's completely right. I'm *not* a celebrity anymore.

But for some reason, I still can't let it go. "What about his article about childhood actors? People still care about people like me."

"Yeah, and people can get your picture off your website. They don't have to sleep with you to get a great story." I can practically see the smoke escaping her ears and nostrils. "Damn it, Siobhan, why did you have to let a great guy like him go?"

"Why do you even care so much?" I demanded. "Why don't you just butt out if it and stop trying to set me up with every guy you meet?"

"Because, Siobhan, I actually give a fuck about you! It

seems like I'm the only one in this room who actually cares."

"What the hell does that mean?" I growl. "Are you saying I don't give a shit about my own well-being?"

"Yeah, Siobhan, that's what I'm saying."

"Well, news flash, Juliet. I don't need a guy in my life to be happy."

"You may not need a guy, but you need Jacob."

What does *that* mean? "I was fine before he came along."

She lowers her voice a bit. "Maybe Jacob needs you."

"Why are you so adamant about this?" I demand. "You don't care how I feel, because you've already taken Jacob's side. It feels like you're only pushing this to make yourself feel good about actually making a relationship work for once."

She winces. Holy crap. I hit a nerve hard on that one. I don't think I've ever insulted Juliet like that before.

"You will not make this about me, Siobhan. At least I *have* relationships."

I roll my eyes. "A one-night stand is not a relationship."

"I said this isn't about me!" she shouts. "This is about you and Jacob. He's the perfect guy for you."

Back to Jacob now. Yes, I have a few things I'd like to say about him.

"I can't trust him. What about the kid he never told me about?"

Her brow furrows. She doesn't know about his kid, either?

"You mean Ben?" she asks.

Okay, so she does know about his kid.

"Yeah," I say like it's a no-brainer.

"Learn to give people a chance, Siobhan. That's not *his* kid, and he's not writing a story about you."

I freeze and then blink a few times, stunned as if someone just slapped me out of nowhere.

"That's... not his kid?" I ask slowly.

The little boy looked just like him.

"That's his sister's kid. Jennifer and Ben just moved to the city and are staying with Jacob until she gets a job and a place of her own."

Oh.

I stumble backward, until the back of my knees hit the couch. I sink down onto it.

So Jacob didn't cheat on anyone? Jen is his sister? Ben is his nephew?

"Why does he leave early from every date, then?" I wonder. It's like I'm trying to find a reason not to be with him.

"Because he has to babysit his nephew while his sister is out interviewing and looking at apartments. That's why he doesn't come into work until the afternoon."

The realization of what's going on strikes me even harder, and my chest compresses.

"Why isn't a guy like him already married?" I'm trying to come up with every excuse I can, because I just can't accept that this might actually work out. To be honest, I'm terrified of it.

"He went traveling for two years and has been focusing on his career for the better part of a decade. He's not prepared for marriage!"

"If he's such a great guy, why aren't you with him?" I snarl.

Her voice softens, and she seems taken aback as if the answer is so simple. "Because he's supposed to be with you."

I don't say anything for about a minute. Juliet stares at me, waiting for a response.

"Why didn't he tell me any of this?" I finally say.

"Because it's not important, Siobhan. What's important right now is that you're doing everything you can to push this great guy away because you're so afraid to fall in love with someone."

She finally came out and said it. Tears fall down my face as I realize that she's right. I made a horrible mistake.

I know it's not Jacob's fault that I reacted the way I did. It was my fear of falling in love—the realization that I loved this man—that I had to sabotage it for myself and turn the situation into something it wasn't.

My heart turns within my chest, sinking, and I bitterly hate myself right now.

"You're right," I admit. "You're completely right."

Shock crosses Juliet's face. She never expected me to confess to it.

"I must have went looking for a reason not to be with him," I say. "I was so happy, but I'm terrified of love."

I look up at her, begging her to rescue me. "I don't know what to do."

Juliet sits next to me on the couch and pulls me into her. "It's going to be all right."

"I should have listened, but I'm so goddamn stubborn." I burry my face into her shoulder, and my body quivers. "I should talk to him."

"I don't know if that's a good idea," she says.

"Why not?"

"You really hurt him when you left the gallery. He said, and I quote, *That girl needs to get her shit together. I don't think it's going to work out between us.* Siobhan, you hurt him. You hurt him bad."

"There has to be something I can do," I insist. I'm the one who created this mess. I have to fix it.

"I think you're going to need a bit more than a quick visit to his apartment to fix this," she advises.

"What am I supposed to do, then?" I whisper.

She shakes her head. "I really don't know."

My shoulders fall, and I stare down at my hands. "I'm such an idiot."

"No, Siobhan." She rubs my shoulder. "Please don't be so hard on yourself."

"I don't even know what's wrong with me."

She stares at me for a few moments before saying, "You're hurt. That's not your fault, but you can't keep hurting *yourself* just because someone hurt you."

"How do I do that when I don't even understand myself? Half the time, I don't know why I'm hurting."

"I think you understand more than you're willing to admit," Juliet says softly.

I mull over her words for several long minutes. "I want to fix this."

"And I want to help," she offers.

I shake my head. "This isn't your mess to fix. Right now, I just need some time to think it over."

She nods. "Take all the time you need."

I climb off the couch and carry myself to my bedroom. The task is difficult, but I eventually make it to the door. I turn back to her, my hand on the frame of my door.

"Thanks, Juliet," I say, forcing the corners of my mouth to turn up in an apologetic smile. "For everything."

CHAPTER TWENTY-ONE

I WAKE up early enough that it's still dark in my room. The city's not quite ready for another day, but I get out of bed anyway. I shower, blow dry my hair, and slip on my favorite jeans and a dark red top. I put on some makeup and give myself an encouraging smile in the mirror.

Juliet isn't awake yet when I leave the apartment. I purposely leave before she wakes so that she can't talk me out of it or give me advice that I don't need.

I slowly make my way to Jacob's place. I know I'm subconsciously stalling the visit as my feet move slowly against the pavement, but my persistence to win this guy's heart back pushes me along. I really don't know what else to do but talk to him. I deleted his number already, and I really don't want to do this over the phone anyway.

I want desperately to make this work between us as I think back on how nice he was to me and how much fun I had with him, but something deep inside of me is still completely frightened of the outcome. I try my best to suppress my anxiety along the walk, but the tension throughout my body is undeniable.

I walk up the stairs as another resident is exiting the building. I quicken my pace up the last few steps and catch the door before it closes. Once at his door, I simply stare at it for a few moments, collecting myself again. When I finally feel ready, I knock.

It takes a few moments, but then I hear shuffling behind the door. It swings open.

Jacob stands in the doorway in jeans and a blue t-shirt. His hair is tidy, and he looks more attractive than I remember. I catch a whiff of his scent as the aroma swiftly moves past me. I want to bury my head in his shoulder and inhale his scent while his arms are wrapped around me.

He seems surprised to see me, but his expression quickly turns hostile. My heart sinks.

"Jacob, I am really sorry," I say in a broken tone. I mean to speak confidently, but seeing him standing in front of me turns my whole body to mush. I hate that I hurt him.

He glances nervously back into his apartment, then back at me. "Jen and Benjamin are still asleep in their room. Mind if we take a walk?"

His suggestion is friendly, but his tone is anything but. His face remains static, unmoving with his words, and it's all very difficult to decipher.

"Sure," I agree. I back away from the door to let him exit.

Neither of us talk until we're out of the building. The

air is a bit cool this morning. I cross my arms around my chest, but I think it's more to make myself feel smaller. I certainly feel about an inch tall in this moment.

"I was way out of line," I start.

"Yeah, you were," he snaps at me, and then he takes a quick breath. I can tell he didn't mean for his tone to come across so harsh.

"I completely misjudged you," I admit. "I guess I was just frightened. I'm not good with relationships."

He gives a bit of a laugh. "Siobhan, no one is good with relationships. It's the trust we put in people that make things work, and I'm not entirely sure that you're ready to put your trust in me."

His words bite.

"I want to be," I insist.

"I don't think a quick visit to my apartment is going to fix this," he says, and I'm instantly reminded of Juliet and the way she said the same thing last night. Jacob's head stays low, and his hands are tucked away in his pockets as we walk.

"How do I know that I can trust *you*, Siobhan?" He stops and turns to me, staring me straight in the eyes. I have a hard time holding his gaze. "It seems you're trying to find every reason possible not to be with me. I'm not sure you're honestly ready for this."

Fear grips my insides, and my voice comes out small. "I'm not sure I am, either. But I want to try."

Jacob sighs. "I appreciate that you're trying, but it's not enough if you aren't ready. I don't want us to hurt each other. You should go home and really think about this, for your own sake. Once you're ready, and if you still want me, then we can talk."

His tone isn't angry or malicious, but he turns away from me and walks back to his apartment as if it will help his words sink in.

"I'm really sorry," I call out to him, but he's already inside the building before he can hear it.

I royally screwed up. I'm afraid nothing I do can fix this.

CHAPTER TWENTY-TWO

WHEN I ARRIVE BACK at the apartment, Juliet is awake and has her paint supplies out. Her plastic tarp is spread across the floor, and her easel sits in front of her.

"How'd it go?" she asks, not taking her eyes off her painting. "I assume you went to talk to Jacob."

How does she pick up on things so quickly?

"I'm not really sure," I reply in an empty tone. "He didn't yell at me, but I didn't exactly win him back."

"I told you that you wouldn't," she says, finally lifting her gaze to mine. "You made him out to be the villain, when all he did was love you."

"I know. He says I need to try harder. Juliet, what does that mean?" I look to her for guidance, hoping she'll tell me exactly what to do. She's usually so good at it.

She pauses from her painting for a moment. "You need to prove that you're ready to love him, but I can't tell you what that looks like because that's up to *you*."

My shoulders fall. "Maybe that's the problem," I say slowly. "Maybe I'm *not* ready."

The realization is like a punch to the gut. I know everything that happened was all because I wasn't ready to love him, and I found a reason to push him away, but it's more than that.

It isn't that he's too good to be true. It's that I'm not willing to believe it.

I whirl back toward the door I just came through.

"Where are you going?" Juliet calls.

"Out." I slam the door behind me.

I don't really know where I'm going, but I need to move.

I thought a walk might clear my head, but if anything, my mind is racing. I don't really pay attention to where I'm going—I just let my feet lead the way.

I find myself standing in front of the yoga studio where I take classes, though I don't go inside. I guess subconsciously I know I need to relax.

After pacing in front of the studio for a few minutes, I breathe a heavy sigh and enter the coffee shop next door. I order a cappuccino, then sink dejectedly into a booth in the corner. I stare down at my coffee without taking a sip.

How could I have ruined something so great? Jacob didn't deserve any of this...

Worst of all, I fear I don't deserve *him*.

"It's going to be okay," a small voice says.

I look up, and my heart stalls in my chest. On the TV near my booth, I see a child's face staring back at me.

Something about the voice sounds familiar, but I don't recognize the actress at first. She has my eyes and shares the same pouty bottom lip, but I feel so disconnected from her that it takes me a moment to realize... she's *me*.

I've seen my movies before, but I've managed to go nearly twenty years without revisiting them. I recognize the movie, but my memory is hazy. I recall the set, but I barely remember filming this scene.

It's *Celina the Detective*, and it's right at the part where she finds her neighbor on the floor in her kitchen after having a heart attack. Celina has called an ambulance, but music crescendos as she waits for the paramedics to arrive.

She holds her neighbor's hand and stares into the camera as she says, "I know you're afraid, but I'm not, because I believe in you."

Tears well in my eyes. In that moment, it feels like she's speaking to *me*—like *I'm* speaking to me.

I remember what it was like back then, believing that anything was possible. I remember believing that love was real.

What happened to me?

My phone starts to vibrate, startling me. I check the screen to see it's my mother. I choke back the tears, then answer.

"Hi, Mom," I say, my voice cracking.

"Siobhan," she greets brightly. "Did your sister send you a photo of her dress?"

"Yeah, she did."

"Good. I wanted to get your opinion on something."

I sigh. "Now's not a good time, Mom."

My mother's voice softens. "Siobhan, what's wrong?"

"It's nothing," I say, but I quickly catch myself in the lie. "I'm just... having a hard day. Mom, why did I quit acting?"

She goes silent for a beat. She has to know something's up if I'm bringing up my acting career. I almost never talk about it.

"You don't remember?" she asks.

"I remember some of it," I admit. "But I was so young."

"You started acting because you were having fun," Mom says. "But then you just... stopped."

"I know I stopped acting, but why?" I wonder.

"No, honey... you stopped having fun. The acting classes, the rehearsals, the filming schedules—it all became too demanding. Your father and I were there to support you every step of the way, but then you said you were done, and we never signed another contract."

"Sometimes it doesn't feel like it ended," I tell her. "We stopped signing contracts, but people kept calling for interviews. I couldn't go places with kids my own age without them recognizing me."

My mother sighs. "Sometimes I wish we'd never let you act. I'm sorry you didn't get the normal childhood you deserve."

"It's not your fault, Mom," I insist. "I'm the one who wanted to do it."

She chuckles lightly. "There was no stopping you,

either. When you put your mind to something, you're going to achieve it no matter what."

I drop my gaze. "I don't feel like I've achieved anything, though. I hit my peak at seven years old."

"That's not true. You moved to New York, like you always wanted. You got your degree, and you built a thriving business. You're only twenty-six, Siobhan. You have so many more years to do whatever you want."

Silence settles across the line as I think about what she said. "I guess that's true. I *did* do everything I set out to do. But it doesn't feel like it matters. Everyone has a degree."

"Not everyone," Mom presses. "Besides, it's not about your accomplishment being one of a kind—it's about what you bring to it that makes it special."

"But Mom, you never celebrated my accomplishments."

"What do you mean?"

"You and Dad didn't come to my college graduation."

"You told us not to," Mom reminds me. "I was going to fly out to New York, while Dad stayed in L.A. for Mackenzie. You said you'd already graduated once, and that we should be there for your sister, like we'd been at your high school graduation."

Her confession tickles a memory I'd long since forgotten. I must've said that and not really meant it at the time.

"You never praised me for my movies," I say.

"Of course we praised you, Siobhan. Every day. We went home after every audition or rehearsal telling you that you did such a good job. You don't remember?"

I sniffle. "I remember people telling me I was a terrible actress. I remember being told I was ugly, and that I didn't deserve the roles I got. I remember being yelled at for forgetting lines. I remember crying after my last premier when the critics said I wasn't going to make it in Hollywood."

"Oh, honey. I never knew you'd read that review. Your father and I never wanted you to see that. Is that why you quit?"

I shake my head. "I don't know, to be honest. I thought the world hated me, so I thought I had to hate myself, too."

"Siobhan, I'm *so* sorry," Mom apologizes. "You never should've had to go through that."

My hand shakes, and I grip my coffee to steady it. "I can't change the past, Mom. So what do I do now?"

She pauses for a beat, before saying, "You change the future."

My mother's words leave me with a lot to think about. I say goodbye, and as soon as I hang up, I open a note on my phone. I begin typing.

I am Not Who They Say I Am

By Siobhan Spencer

I grew up thinking I was playing characters—that it was all for fun and that at the end of the day, I could come home and be myself. But I was just a kid. I never knew who I was, and so I all I knew how to do was became the characters I played.

I never got the chance to figure myself out. I was so used to stepping into these different roles, that I took on the role I thought people wanted me to. They said I was talentless, and I believed it. They said I was ugly, so I stopped looking in the mirror. They told me I didn't deserve my accomplishments, and so I never celebrated them. They told me I was nothing exceptional, so I settled for mediocre.

Everyone wanted me to be something I wasn't, but I never asked myself who I wanted to become. All I wanted was for someone to recognize me for me.

And the one person who could never do that... was myself.

I am Siobhan Spencer. I am a daughter, a friend, and an artist. I'm passionate and driven. I am caring, and I love my friends and family deeply. I am articulate and compassionate, creative and spontaneous. I am dedicated and loyal, organized and kind.

I am whatever I choose to be.

They said I'd never play a leading lady, but they were wrong. I realize now that no one is going to give me this role, because I have to write the damn script myself.

A tear slips down my cheek as I reread what I wrote. I don't hit publish on this one, because I don't need anyone else's opinions. I already have everything I need.

"Siobhan?" a familiar voice comes from beside me. I look up to see Abby holding a coffee.

Jasmine comes up behind her, and worry crosses her features. "Are you okay?"

I wipe the tear from my cheek. "I'm doing much better, thanks."

I pause for a beat before adding, "Are you two ready for that girl talk?"

Smiles light up their faces. Jasmine and Abby sit, and I dish out every detail of what happened between Jacob and me.

"Are you going to try to win him back?" Abby asks after I finish.

Jasmine gasps, like she just had the best idea. "You could pull off a big romantic gesture, like in the movies. Throw rocks at his window, or hire a flash mob."

I chuckle. "I don't think winning him back is the answer. I don't know how our story ends yet, but I think I know what I need to do."

"What's that?" Abby asks curiously.

"I need to show him who I truly am."

CHAPTER TWENTY-THREE

I TELL Juliet about my plan, and she's completely on board. When Friday night arrives, I feel the nerves rising in my gut.

There's an art reception at Watson's Gallery tonight. Juliet rearranged the schedule to make the event bigger than ever, and I promoted it on my blog. I even wrote up a press release and submitted it to small newspapers across the city. I managed to get a few small news crews to agree to cover the reception. Juliet spent the week trying to keep the secret from Jacob.

"You're going to do great," I tell myself in the mirror. I dress in the same red dress I wore last weekend, the beautiful red one that shows off my back. The smile across my face shows my dimples, my eyes are bright, and I look happy. "Just be yourself and speak the truth."

Before I turn away from the mirror, I tell myself one last thing. "Siobhan, you look beautiful."

For the first time, I completely believe it.

Juliet and I arrive at the reception before it starts, and she hides me in one of the back rooms so Jacob won't spot me.

As people start arriving, I take a quick peek out into the vast room, and I'm shocked by what I see. I've been to two opening receptions at this gallery before, and there weren't very many people here at either one compared to this. Tonight, there are more people than the gallery can hold. A line stretches far out onto the street.

I take a deep, calming breath, and my nerves subside.

When it's time, Juliet heads up to the microphone. She looks beautiful and poised standing in front of all these people. What I would normally channel as jealousy for her beauty turns into a sense of admiration for her.

"You are here tonight not to view a piece of artwork, but to experience it," Juliet announces.

The entire room goes silent. I can't see Jacob in the crowd, but I know he's here. He helped organize the rest of the exhibit.

"Tonight, we aren't going to focus on these works of art on the walls, but rather, we're here to witness a different type of intricate work of art," Juliet continues. "It's not in a medium that we can see or touch. Love is displayed in a much more complicated manner. Tonight, I would like to welcome my very good friend to the stage. Please put your hands together for Siobhan Spencer."

Juliet gestures to the back of the room, where I emerge from my hiding spot. All eyes turn to look at me. The people are packed in here like sardines, but they somehow manage to part and make way for me. My hands shake nervously, but when I reach the stage and begin speaking into the microphone, my voice is surprisingly even.

I've prepared a speech, but none of it is coming back to me, so I begin to improvise.

"I'd like to start with a show of hands," I begin. "How many of you have heard the name Siobhan Spencer before?"

More people than I expect raise their hands. I know most of them are my local followers.

"So maybe you don't all know my name. Let's try a different show of hands. How many of you recognize me?" To my amazement, over half of the crowd raises their hands. I can tell the audience is intrigued. As my gaze travels around the room, I notice the film crews in the back, and I'm grateful they're here. I want my message to be heard everywhere.

"I was once an actress. I starred in the movies *Celina the Detective*, *Taking Reservations*, and *Beyond the Meadow*." A few voices rise within the crowd as more people realize who I am based on the movie titles.

"I'm not going to sugar-coat the truth—I'm screwed the fuck up. I used to think that my childhood didn't affect me, but looking back, I realize that what felt normal wasn't normal at all. Things I thought I'd forgotten about, or situations I'd shrugged off, had shaped who I am."

I take a deep breath, preparing for my next confession. "I became someone who was afraid to fall in love."

I remember telling Jacob on our first date that I was fearless, but I realize now how wrong I was.

"People have judged me my entire life. First, they told me I was special, and then all of a sudden, I wasn't. People called me ugly, a bad actress, and a spoiled child, even though I wasn't any of those things. While deep down I knew that, I let these people get to me."

Everyone in the room watches me intently.

"Then it wasn't the media judging me. Instead, judgment came from my fellow classmates, my parents' friends, and my teachers. Either people wanted to be my friend because they thought I was special, or they didn't like me because they hated the movie I was in. Nobody seemed to like me for who I really was, and because of this, I didn't think anyone could truly fall in love with me. I didn't believe I could love anyone back."

As the words tumble out of me, it's like a huge weight has been lifted off my shoulders. I finally find Jacob's face in the crowd. He's shocked, and he stands unmoving as he stares up at me. He looks glorious—better than I remember.

"That is until a few weeks ago when I met the most amazing man." My eyes lock upon him.

The crowd follows my gaze to stare at Jacob. The people around him begin backing away until he's alone in his space. He doesn't even notice the crowd shift because he's staring up at me, though his expression is fixed and difficult to read.

"I didn't want to admit it to myself, but I fell in love," I continue. "I was so afraid of falling in love that I found reasons why I shouldn't. I convinced myself that there was no way this man was right for me, and I didn't listen to him when he tried to tell me the truth. I was so afraid of him judging me for my past that I turned around and did the exact same thing to him. I'm ashamed of myself for it."

I hear a mummer spread throughout the crowd.

"But I've realized that I don't have to accept the person I've become," I state. "I can choose to be someone else. I can choose to love, and I can choose to let someone love me."

I stop talking to the crowd and instead focus my conversation solely at Jacob. "It wasn't fair to you, Jacob. From the moment I met you, I saw this light within you that intrigued me as much as it terrified me. The way you listened to me and let me make my own decisions... it was so different from anything I'd experienced before. You trusted me to be myself, and even though I was afraid, I felt like I could be. But I didn't know who I was, and I'm still learning. I know that when I'm with you, you bring out the best in me. I smile and laugh, and I feel so carefree, like for the first time in my life, I don't have to hide. Every moment we're together, I feel like I'm discovering love for the first time."

I draw a shaky breath. "I feel like we'll never run out of things to talk about, like we'll always have stories to tell. I told you once that I didn't want to tell my own story, but I realize now that I was afraid of it. I was afraid of what it meant about me, and I was afraid of what you'd think. If you don't want to be part of my story, I understand. But I think it's time that I start telling it."

I steady my tone. "From the bottom of my heart, I am sorry, and I hope that you can forgive me."

For a moment, I think that he's going to turn away and leave. And maybe that's okay. He doesn't owe me anything. But if he chooses to walk away, I hope he knows one thing.

"Jacob Bishop, I am desperately in love with you," I confess.

Jacob finally blinks, and he takes a few steps forward. The crowd splits as he makes his way to the stage. I can't read the expression on his face.

Jacob takes my hands in his. "For the longest time, I didn't know what I wanted. Then I met you, and it felt like every indecision had led me right to your doorstep. You know what you want, and you go after it—even the simplest, spontaneous things like a photo booth. And every time, you bring me along for the ride. You talk about books and movies like they're a part of you, and you see art every-where you go. I've never been around someone who I could talk to so freely about the things I care about, or someone who saw art in the skyline the way I did. You're open to compromise, and you're so passionate about lifting up other artists. Siobhan, I don't care that you're afraid. What matters is that you chose to face it. Maybe you haven't overcome it just yet, but you're the kind of girl who will achieve anything she desires."

Jacob steps up to the microphone. "I just want you all to know..."

I can feel everyone in the room holding their breath. I know I am.

"That this is the woman of my dreams," he finishes, pointing at me with a magnificent grin on his face.

The breath I was holding releases in a wave of relief. All my nerves are replaced with fluttering joy.

Jacob wraps his arms around me, and his lips pause an inch away from mine. "Will you take me along for one more ride?"

I nod eagerly. "Yes."

Jacob grips me tightly and swings me back into a dip and plants a long, hard kiss on my lips in front of everyone. I'm glowing as fireworks go off in my stomach and the crowd cheers.

His lips pull away from mine, and he whispers in my ear, "I'm glad you gave me a second chance."

"You never needed a second chance," I whisper back. "I'm the one who needed the second chance. Thank you for giving it to me."

He crinkles his nose. "To be fair, I wasn't very clear about my sister. That must have looked really bad."

I shake my head. "You have nothing to apologize for."

He shrugs. "Then I guess we can call it even."

Jacob pulls me into another kiss, and the crowd gives us a thunderous round of applause.

CHAPTER TWENTY-FOUR

JACOB and I make our way off the stage holding hands, and people stop to congratulate us.

"What a touching work of art," one man says.

Another woman touches me on the shoulder. "That was beautiful."

I guide Jacob over to Juliet so I can thank her for all the hard work she put into this. Danielle Watson, the gallery owner, who is a thin, older woman with long grey hair, is talking to Juliet.

"I am very pleased the way you handled this, Juliet. Look at all the exposure we got tonight," Danielle says, gesturing to the crowd around her with excitement in her eyes.

When she leaves, I embrace Juliet. "Thank you for everything you've done for us. I'm really sorry about the way I acted. I was a real bitch."

She wrinkles her nose. "Yeah, you kind of were," she admits, but I'm not bothered by it. It's true.

Juliet and Jacob embrace as well, my hand still connected to his. "Thank you for everything," Jacob says.

"Didn't I tell you two you'd make a perfect couple?" she boasts, and we both roll our eyes at her. "I'll see you two kids around," she says as she heads off to tend to other guests.

Once she's gone, I turn to Jacob. "I really am sorry."

"Don't be," he tells me as he smiles down at me. "I can see where you're coming from, especially that thing with my sister. I can see how that looked. I remember telling you she just moved back to the city, but I guess I forgot to mention she was living with me. It never seemed important. I'm sorry."

He grabs on to a piece of my hair hanging by my face and tucks it behind my ear. "I can imagine love is hard for you, and I want to be there to get you through it."

My God, I could not have fallen in love with a better man.

"Why are you so understanding and nice?" I ask. "No one has ever treated me the way you do."

"Siobhan," he says, as if the answer is staring me straight in the face. "I knew you were the girl for me when you walked into Michelle's. Something about you just... made me want to care."

I recall the way I stared down at my hands in the restaurant, unwilling to meet his eyes, and the way he pulled up my chin and charmed me.

"I've been really curious about something," I say. "How come you didn't know who I was? Didn't you have a TV?"

He shrugs. "I didn't watch a lot of television. I was the kid who drew pictures and made finger paintings for entertainment. Photography and painting are what really interested me."

I study him for a moment, and I know without a doubt I can trust him. More than that, I can *love* him. I'm captivated by his eyes, addicted to his touch, and in love with the things he shares with me, like the Ferris wheel ride.

"Oh, I have something to show you," I remember, and I pull my phone from the small black handbag I'm carrying and flip through it. Once I find what I'm looking for, I hand him the phone. It's the photo I took of the Ferris wheel when it had its lights on. "I used the tips you gave me."

He stares at the photo. "This is beautiful," he says, and then my phone begins vibrating in his hand.

Seeing that I have an incoming call, he hands the phone back to me. It's my sister.

"Hello," I answer.

"Hi!" she squeals. "I just wanted you to know that we set an official date for the wedding. We're getting married on December nineteenth."

"That's great!" I say honestly. "I'm really happy for you."

I look up at Jacob and mouth the words, *My sister's getting married.*

After a moment, I ask, "Hey, Mackenzie, will I be able to bring a date to your wedding?"

"Of course," she squeaks. "Are you saying you have a boyfriend?"

My eyes lock on Jacob, and I smirk. "I have an incredible boyfriend."

Jacob grins at me.

"That's awesome!" my sister exclaims. "You *better* bring him to the wedding, because I want to meet him. Congratulations!"

"Hey, Mackenzie, I'm kind of busy right now. Can I call you later?"

"Sure, but before you go, I have a quick question for you."

"Yeah?"

She pauses for a moment, and then squeals as quickly as humanly possible, "Will you be my maid of honor?"

I'm thrilled by the invitation. "I'd love that."

"Great! I'll call you later. Bye."

As I hang up, a man with a camera comes up to us. He must be part of one of the news crews. He's very tall and attractive, almost model-like with wispy blonde hair and strong muscles. He looks like the type of guy Juliet would date.

"Mind if I snap a photo of the happy couple?" the guy asks, and Jacob and I strike a pose, his arm draped around me.

"Thanks," he says as he turns away from us, searching for other shots he can take.

"So, I'm invited to your sister's wedding?" Jacob asks.

"You sure are," I answer.

I hear the click of heels from behind me.

"Hey, guys," a woman's voice says, greeting us.

I turn around, and I recognize the woman.

"Hey, Jen," Jacob greets as they embrace.

"Hi," I say warily. She must have thought I was crazy to think they were together.

"That was a beautiful speech, Siobhan," she compliments as she comes in closer to embrace me.

For a moment, I'm shocked, but I quickly relax.

She takes a step back. "It's about time my big brother finds a girl."

"I'm really sorry about everything," I say. "You know, that I thought Ben was Jacob's kid."

She waves a hand. "They look enough alike that it wouldn't be the first time."

The visitations don't end there. Once Jen walks away, Jasmine and Abby greet us.

"Oh my God, Siobhan," Abby cries—literally, there are tears falling from her eyes, but she wipes them away. "That really was the ultimate love display."

"I wish a guy would do something like that for me," Jasmine agrees, embracing me.

I thank them for coming, and after they leave, Jacob and I stroll the gallery, taking in all the glorious works of art.

"So..." Jacob says, elongating the word. "What exactly *don't* I know about you?"

I think for a few moments, really trying to rack my brain for an answer. "I think you know about everything now. No! Wait." I stop in my tracks. "My middle name is Anne."

He looks at me from the side, biting his lip. "Actually, I did know that one."

What? I never told him that.

"Wikipedia," he explains. Of course Wikipedia would know my middle name.

"Well, I don't know yours," I tell him, remembering how difficult it was to find him online without a middle name.

He smiles, then answers. "Cole."

I take in this new information. "Jacob Cole Bishop," I repeat. "Anything else I don't know?"

He plants himself in front of me, placing his hands on each of my shoulders. "That I am utterly captivated by you," he whispers as he leans down and presses a kiss to my lips. "That I think your eyes are gorgeous, and that I love your lips."

What? He runs his thumb across my pouty bottom lip as he says this.

"That you taste magnificent," he confesses.

My God, is he trying to seduce me? And which part of me is he talking about? He moves in closer, and I take in his scent. I want him, right here, right now. I bite my bottom lip and stare him up and down. Jacob has me in a trance, and I can't control myself. After a moment, I regain my strength and give him a friendly push.

"Not here, Jacob," I scold playfully.

He raises his eyebrows and whispers seductive words into my ear.

I laugh. "There are people around."

We stay for the rest of the reception, and I end up meeting a bunch of my followers. Soon, though, the crowd begins to clear. We're ready to go when Juliet comes up to us, her arm wrapped around the sexy photographer's.

"Hey, guys, I won't make it home tonight," she informs us, batting her eyes at the gorgeous man beside her. "You two have fun," she says as she waves goodbye.

"We will," I promise, waving after her. I look up at Jacob. "Well, shall we?"

He nods. "We shall."

My heart soars as we stroll out of the gallery and make our way back to my apartment.

It doesn't even take a moment after we enter the door before his hands are already around me. I kick my heels off, hike my dress up, and wrap my legs around him. Our lips lock together.

He carries me into my bedroom and gently helps me out of my dress before placing me on the bed. He wraps me in his arms and kisses me. He tastes *so* sweet.

I pull back. "I don't want to hide anything from you. A guy kissed me last week. I didn't want him to, but I thought you should know."

Concern washes over his features. "Are you okay?"

I nod. "Yeah, I am."

He brushes the hair out of my eyes. "Then that's in the past."

Relief washes over me. "I want to let go of the past. From this moment on, I want to start fresh."

Jacob lifts my chin, forcing my eyes to meet his. "Siobhan, if this is what you want, then I promise you that nothing will ever be the same."

It's everything I need to hear, and I throw my arms around his neck and drag him on top of me. He relaxes into me, and the passion between us is unmatched. Waves of pleasure pulse through our bodies over and over, until we fall to the bed in exhaustion.

We lay awake the rest of the night cuddled close. We divulge every single detail of our pasts, and we make plans for our future.

For the first time, I actually feel fearless.

EPILOGUE

A KNOCK COMES at the door, and I turn from the bright lights reflecting off the mirrors. "Come in," I call.

Makeup artists surround Juliet and me, and the hair stylist spritzes my curls with hairspray. The door opens, and my heart leaps when I see Jacob standing there. It's been three years, and my stomach still flip-flops every time he enters the room. He's dressed in a suit, and his hair is combed back. He looks sexier than ever.

"Are you ready?" he asks with a charming smile. "It's almost time to go."

"We'll be right out, Mister Bishop," my publicist Amelia tells him.

I stand. "It's okay. My husband can come in."

Jacob enters the dressing room, and he takes my hands, his thumb roaming over my wedding ring. I tilt my chin up, and he places a tender kiss on my lips.

"Save it for the red carpet," Juliet jokes.

I smirk. "I'm not saving anything. I could kiss this man all day."

Jacob smiles down at me. "Then we better get started now."

He kisses me again.

"All right," Amelia says, stepping forward. "If you're trying to get us out the door, it's working. Juliet is right. Save it for the cameras. The news crews are going to want to see this—the starring lady and her muse."

The stylist crew moves to pack up, but Jacob doesn't tear his eyes off me. "I can't believe you did it."

"*We* did it," I correct him.

"Yeah, but it was your script," he says. "This movie never would've been made without you."

I chuckle. "Nor without you. You're not just my muse —you and Juliet directed the whole arts department!"

Jacob beams. "We all make a good team, don't we?"

"I'd say so. According to Amelia, the movie's projected to open at number one at the box office," I say.

Amelia steps in. "It's show time! Let's get our stars to the limo."

I slip my elbow through Jacob's and hold my head up confidently as he leads me to our limo. I climb inside and stare out the window as the driver takes us through the streets New York City. I can't believe how far I've come. It feels surreal to be back in the spotlight—not just as an actress this time, but as a writer.

I wasn't expecting my movie to garner the attention it has. I thought my script might pique the interest of a few small studios, so I was surprised when my agent called to tell me it'd entered a major bidding war between several large film companies.

The winning studio signed me later that year to play the lead role. After months of revisions, production preparations, filming, editing, and marketing, my film is finally premiering tonight.

I never thought something like this would happen to me, because I always believed I was nothing special.

The thing is, I've always been extraordinary. I just didn't let myself shine.

Tonight, I shimmer brighter than ever before.

The limo stops, and Jacob opens my door and offers his hand. I take it and step onto the red carpet.

Thundering applause fills the night, and flashing lights shine from all angles. My red dress glimmers against the glistening bulbs. A wide smile spreads across my face as I wave to the eager crowd.

"Siobhan!" people call my name. "Look over here, Siobhan!"

I glance over my shoulder, and a photographer snaps my photo.

"Siobhan Spencer!" a fan cries from the other side of velvet ropes. "Can I have your autograph?"

I take the pen from their hand and sign a photo they've brought along.

"This way, Siobhan!" someone calls, though there are so many people that I can't tell who's talking.

We follow my team down the red carpet. Jacob taps my

shoulder and points. I look up, and I nearly topple over when I see my face smiling from a billboard. Jacob had taken the photo for the movie poster himself.

"Can you believe this is happening?" he asks.

I glance around, taking in the sound of cheering voices and the *snap* of the cameras. A warm sense of belonging fills my chest. "You know what? I really can believe it."

We're ushered to a mark on the carpet facing the photographers. Jacob wraps an arm around me, and I strike my best pose.

My eyes scan the reporters, until they land upon Amelia. Her eyes widen, and she gestures, as if to say, *Now's the time.*

I turn to Jacob, grinning up at him. "They love you."

"*I* love *you*," he says, before pressing his lips to mine.

The cameras flash as the crowd goes wild.

My head spins, and I force my pulse to slow as I draw away. "That's going to make the front page."

He smirks. "I'm counting on it."

Amelia gestures to us again, and we continue down the red carpet. Another man takes his place in front of the photographers, and the crowd screams for my costar.

I see our director up ahead, and I rush over to her. "Elizabeth!"

She turns to me with a huge smile on her face. "Siobhan! You look amazing."

I pull her into a hug. "Not as amazing as you. You haven't aged a day since I met you."

Elizabeth scoffs. "Honey, that was over twenty years ago."

"And yet there's a reason you were on the cover of a magazine earlier this year," I tell her.

She laughs. "It's funny, you know. The headlines used to talk about Elizabeth River—movie star. Now they're writing about a movie I've *directed*. I've always wanted to sit in the director's chair, and there's no better script I could've directed than yours, Siobhan."

"I'm just glad we got to work together again," I tell her.

"I promise, this film won't be our last project together," she says.

"Siobhan!" Someone calls my name, and I'm led over to a film crew. A woman in a beautiful blue gown holds a microphone.

"Siobhan, what message do you want people to take away from this film?" she asks, before aiming the microphone at me.

"Never be afraid to fall in love." I shoot a glance at Jacob. "You never know what's waiting for you on the other side."

The interviewer only gets a few minutes with me before I'm ushered in front of another camera. I beam the whole time, feeling a weightless sensation in my chest as I take it all in.

Soon, we enter the theatre, where I see my family has already taken their seats. I managed to get tickets for them, and they light up when they see me. Mackenzie and her husband Derek stand up and start clapping.

I do a little spin down the aisle, then bow at them. My sister whistles.

Mine and Jacob's seats are next to them, so we find our way down their row. Mom and Dad stand, and they each pull me into a hug in turn.

"We're so proud of you," Mom says, squeezing me for what feels like a full minute.

"This is a huge accomplishment," Dad adds, and he draws away with tears in his eyes.

"I couldn't have done it without you two," I tell them. "You encouraged me to follow my dreams. None of this would be happening without you."

"We couldn't be happier," Mom says.

Mackenzie hugs me next. "Congratulations! Be honest with me, do I need the tissues? I have a feeling I'm going to cry."

I click my tongue at her. "Spoilers, Mackenzie."

She sticks out her bottom lip, and I laugh as I take my seat.

Jacob drapes his arm around me and leans back proudly. "Let's just say you won't be disappointed."

"He knows the plot twist!" Mackenzie accuses.

I laugh, but I give nothing away.

The lights dim, and Juliet quickly finds her way over to us. "I can't believe this is it!" she squeals.

Music begins to play, and the screen lights up as the opening credits play across the screen. My voice enters the speakers and fills the entire theatre.

A euphoric feeling washes over me. Jacob pulls me closer and kisses the side of my face.

"You okay?" he asks.

I nod eagerly. "Absolutely. I've got the best seat in the entire house."

The music crescendos as the movie title plays across the screen. I can't help but read it out loud, as if to convince myself that I'm not dreaming.

"*In Jacob's Arms*," I whisper, before resting my head on my husband's shoulder. "Right where I'm meant to be."

ABOUT THE AUTHOR

Alicia Rades is a USA Today bestselling author of young adult and new adult paranormal fiction. *In Jacob's Arms* is her only contemporary romance. When she's not dreaming up magical stories, she's either binge-watching Netflix, meditating, or spending time with her family.

www.ingramcontent.com/pod-product-compliance
Lightning Source LLC
Chambersburg PA
CBHW031602310726
48974CB00003B/774